To Pam,
A Wonderful
Person - Love
Teda Taylor Strom

Grandpa's Adventures

by

Veda Taylor Strong

authorHOUSE™

1663 LIBERTY DRIVE, SUITE 200
BLOOMINGTON, INDIANA 47403
(800) 839-8640
WWW.AUTHORHOUSE.COM

First published by AuthorHouse 03/28/05

ISBN: 1-4208-2974-2 (sc)

Library of Congress Control Number: 2005900827

Printed in the United States of America
Bloomington, Indiana

This book is printed on acid-free paper.

PROLOGUE: REMEMBERING

Jane and the kids were on the railroad platform waiting for the Northern Pacific that would be taking them to their new home in Montana. They were surrounded by their many friends. Some came with them from Kansas and others were newer acquaintances they had met in Tacoma.

Suddenly they could hear the lonesome sound of the train as it made the last bend around the mountain. Everyone was trying to hug all at once and shouting their good wishes and good bys.

The children were being pushed up the iron train steps ahead of Jane. She turned around and gave a big wave. They were leaving their life in Tacoma and the life that was woven around John. She turned and went through the door into the coach of the train. The conductor was helping get the children and her situated together with plenty of room for their luggage. It would be a long trip.

The train started moving and the children settled down. Soon they were all asleep. So much had happened and there hadn't been much time for a lot of sleep or rest.

As she sat and listened to the rhythm of the train wheels, her mind started wandering back to the beginning of her life with John. How John told her about his life in the Civil War and his wandering through and after the war ended.

Soon she was absolutely in her own remembering…………

HEADIN' HOME

After the Civil War, John wandered around the country. Like so many from the battlefields, he wasn't sure what he wanted to do. He thought that maybe he'd like to go west, possibly California, Oregon or Washington territories. He had mustered out of the army at Burlington, Tennessee and had been wandering for months, finding odd jobs to keep himself busy, and money to live on. He had been missing his family for a long time and couldn't help but wonder what they were doing and how they were faring. He was growing tired of roaming. Giving into his feeling of home sickness, he decided to head north, leaving the war torn south behind him.

He wondered about Frank and Alfred. Did they make it through the fightin'? His brothers were five and six years older than him and had enlisted in the army when the war started. He hadn't seen them for nearly six years. 'Maybe his folks had some news of 'em.'

His three sisters, Maggie, Gladys and Kate were much younger than him. They were giggling little girls playing with their rag dolls and stuffed animals. The baby, Edward, had turned three years old when John left. The family had always called him 'Eddie'.

Thomas and Mary, John's parents, had moved their family to a town called Sioux City in the state of Iowa. The town shared it's border on the Missouri River with the state of Nebraska on the far bank. The mouth of the Big Sioux River bordered the town to the north. It was named after the Indian tribes in the Dakota territories.

Thomas had farming in his blood. He had grown up as a farmer and was a very good one. He had sold his holdings and had moved from Lorain County, Ohio shortly after John had left to fight. Being a shrewd business man, he had been able to acquire a section of land, including many acres of fertile bottom land at the mouth of the Big Sioux River.

As John rode along, he noticed the rich fields of alfalfa, corn, oats, soybeans and other grains as far as he could see. Large herds of cattle and large hog pens seemed to have their place on many of the farms. Every farm had chickens that ran loose around their coops. All in all, making for a nice laid back peaceful scene.

Riding over a rise, he spied the town. From a distance, he spotted the church steeple, rising up into the clear blue sky. He soon made out a school with a large bell tower on the top, two general stores, one at each end of the main street, large livery stables with what he gathered to be a blacksmith-shop, saloon and a two story hotel with a dining room and a saloon.

Large holding pens were near the train depot where the cattle and hogs were held while waiting to be shipped to market. Cattle were mostly being driven by drovers on cattle drives or by barges on the river. The trains were fairly new contraptions and not yet trusted completely. They were rarely on time and always breaking down with mechanical problems.

As he got closer, he could see that it was a busy place with people everywhere. A boy and his dog were running up the dusty main street, playing with a ball and a hoop. A man with a long beard and a mustache was going into the saloon and two ladies were leaving the White's general store with large parcels in their arms. A new two story structure was being built one street over behind the main street. A bank being built on Main street close to the White's general store. The town promised to be much larger than it was now.

Stopping in front of White's, he got off his horse and wrapped the reins around the railing. His big bay horse looked tired, hot and thirsty. John hoped to get him fed and watered soon. Taking his hat, he tried to beat some of the trail dust off of his clothes. Hopefully, he could get information here. Someone might know of his family.

The store was a large building with a wide wooden porch across the front, complete with a large railing. Large burlap sacks of corn, flour, and sugar barrels, along with large wooden barrels of pickles and crackers set around the front door, spilling into the store itself.

Shelves were lined with canned goods and other food staples that had been brought in by freight wagons.

Entering the store, he noticed a young brunette behind the counter. She was busy putting up a grocery order, writing down each item and price on a sheet of paper, while a woman waited.

While waiting until the young lady was no longer busy, he wandered around the store. A black pot bellied stove sat in the corner of the room. This would keep the store warm when the cold and snow came. Three old gentlemen were sitting around swapping stories and arguing over a checker game that two of the men were engaged in.

"Hello! Nice day!" John said to no one in particular. The old gentlemen nodded to John and then went back to their game of checkers. They weren't being overly friendly. He noticed the leather goods hanging on the wall and two saddles laid out on sawhorses below them. He liked the aroma of the new leather.

In his wonderings, he came to the cloth materials and notions. A little bit of everything from large bolts of gingham for the ladies dresses and cotton lingerie and other things in heavy woolens for winter coats and pants. John had learned to be a tailor in the army and was a very good one. He enjoyed the feel of good cloth.

When he seen that the young lady was no longer busy, he sauntered over to the counter.

Looking up, she asked, "Can I help you? Sorry to keep you waitin'! It can get really busy around here sometimes."

"Hello! I would like a handful of licorice sticks." he answered, fishing in his small leather coin purse for the coins to pay her.

"I'm looking for my folks!" John continued. "I thought that maybe I could get some information on 'em. Have you heard of the Thomas Taylor family? They moved around here a couple years back. I'm their son John! Mustered out of the army in Tennessee and I've been wandering ever' since. Thought it was time that I looked up the folks."

Smiling with pretty dimpled cheeks, she had John wondering if she was spoken for. She wore a brown dress with a white lacy collar. The dress matched her pretty big brown eyes.

"What's your name?" John asked, as he took his change from her.

Her look turned to a look of curiosity.

She knew that she hadn't seen him before. He looked harmless enough. A little bit weather beaten but nice to look at, with a small brown mustache. He stood five feet eight inches tall and had very good manners. 'Nice girls don't give their names but after all, I know his family. What could be the harm in telling him?'

"As it happens, I do know your family. They are our neighbors on the river." She told him as she came out from behind the counter.

She began giving him directions to his folks place.

"I'm sorry to interrupt but how are Ma and Pa doin'? I haven't heard anything for a long time."

"They're fine! Frank and Al are there. Actually we see quite a bit of your family. They are very nice people and wonderful neighbors."

Looking around, John noticed that the store was getting busy again. He didn't want to keep her from her customers for too long. He guessed it was time for him to be on his way.

"I'll be seein' you again soon. Thanks for your help!" John said with a big smile and a wink as he turned towards the door.

'I will be lookin' forward to seein' you again, too.' She thought, hoping that he would be comin' into the store very soon.'

John walked down the steps into the street. Taking the horse's reins, he led the bay to a water trough that was close by. While the bay drank, he looked the town over. It just seemed to be like other towns that were springing up. Like places he had gone through to get here.

Giving the town one last glance, he got on his horse and using the directions that Jane had given him, he headed towards his folks place.

As John got closer to the river, he became awestruck by it's beauty and the activity going on. He decided to check it out. Being alone, he would be able to take his time and explore a little bit.

Getting off his horse and gripping the reins, he found a well worn path leading to the river bank.

'The Missouri River! It is so wide! I guess it must be a half mile wide here! It is breath taking to see how muddy and swift it is.' he thought, as he watched the barges go up and down the river. They carried farm goods, cattle and all types of cargo. Looking down the river, he noticed people boarding a large paddle boat. He could only imagine where they were going or coming from. 'Probably as far away as Montana to the west and meeting up with the Mississippi River at St. Louis, Missouri. Moving as far south as New Orleans and the Gulf of Mexico. Because of the swift under currents, I hear that the river is very unpredictable and can't be trusted.'

Looking off to his right, he saw two young boys sitting on the river bank, fishing. Each boy had a fishing pole fashioned from a small tree limb. With their patched pants and no shoes, they didn't seem to have a care in the world. John figured them to be about eleven years old. He looked at one then the other. It was like mirrored images. "Well! I'll be!" he exclaimed. They were identical twins.

A large dog had been laying asleep between the boys. Opening one eye as John approached, he swished his tail a couple of times and sized him up.

"Howdy! Fishin' any good?" John asked. "Have you caught anythin'?"

"Who are you, Mister?" One of the boys shyly asked.

John introduced himself and then asked who they were.

"My name is Zac." Pointing to his brother, he went on, "This is my brother Nick. Guess you can see that we are twins." Nudging the dog with his toe, he introduced their pet as just 'Dog'. "We live in town. Our Pa's the blacksmith. We come here a lot to fish 'cuz there ain't many people that come around here."

"Fishin's good! Caught a two pound trout a couple days ago. I seen 'em as big as three pounds. Now, there is a special way to catch these."

"Do you wanna learn how? You have to find a clump of bushes and put your line down so it can float 'neath the bank to where the big 'uns are hidin' out." replied the boy named Nick. "It takes a long time to get a nibble and sometimes you can wait all day and not even get a bite. Takes lots of patience!"

"Uh uh! Ma says that you build stories and tell too many tales." corrected Zac. Turning to John, he continued, "He caught a big one but we didn't see a two or three pound 'un'."

Nick pushed Zac and down they went on the grass, rolling over and over a few times. They both sat up laughing.

"Do you wanna do some fishin'?" Zac asked as he started to get up off the ground. "I'll fix you up with a pole."

"Don't get up!" exclaimed John. "I don't have the time right now but if you boys are around in a few days, I will try to find you and we'll do some fishin'. Sounds like lots of fun to me. Haven't been fishin' for a long time!" He reached into his pocket and gave each boy a licorice stick.

Reaching down, he gathered up a handful of rich soil. Smelling the earth, he couldn't help thinking that maybe this would be a good place to settle down and put down roots of his own.

Suddenly, Jane's face appeared in his thoughts. He again wondered if she was spoken for. As soon as he could, he would find out. She was very pretty, and thoughtful. He wanted to get to know her better. He would see how everything went and then he would go back to White's store as soon as he possibly could.

The afternoon was wearing on. Night was approaching. He wasn't sure of his whereabouts, so he decided that he should be on his way before it started getting dark. He didn't want to get turned around and maybe lost. Promising the boys that he would come back, he walked the worn path back the way that he had come. Getting on his horse, he again headed for his folks place.

HOME COMIN'

Down the road, John could see a two story white house with a large front and large back porch. Riding closer, he came to a big gate. Reaching down, he lifted the leather thong from the pole that held it. Pushing the gate open, he rode through, turned around and again reached down and put the thong back over the pole. He then continued on towards the house.

Pretty flowering plants were set around on the front porch and the windows had flower boxes flowing with colorful blooms. Two rocking chairs, carefully centered on the porch, were rocking slightly in the breeze. Several large oak trees were scattered in the yard around the house. Two swings had been hung on the lower limb of one of the trees and they too were swaying in the breeze.

Getting down from the horse, he wrapped the reins around the porch rail. He was just turning around when he heard his mother's voice.

"Who's there? Oh, my goodness! Is that you, John?" They clasped each other in their arms and wept.

"What is goin' on out here?" his father asked as he came out of the house.

"Just look who's come home, Thomas!" Mary exclaimed. "I can hardly believe it."

Thomas grabbed John in a mighty bear hug! Neither man was ashamed of the tears in their eyes!

"We have been so worried about you. Not havin' heard any news, we didn't know if or when we would see you agin'. It is so wonderful to have you home. How are you? Were you hurt? How did you find us?" asked Tom.

"I'll try and answer all your questions. First of all, it's a wonderful feelin' to be here! Seems like many years ago that I seen you. The war was terrible but I wasn't wounded. Them Reb's weren't fast enough

14

to get me." John answered with a chuckle, trying to make light of the ugliness he had left behind. "Stopped at White's general store and Jane White gave me the directions here."

"Jane and her family live just down the road. They are very nice neighbors. You'll be meetin 'em soon, I'm sure. Come into the house! Your brothers and sisters are all here. They'll be surprised and happy to see you!" Mary told him excitedly, "Everybody come here! John's home!"

As John went into the living room, he was hugged by the rest of the family. Frank and Al had just come in from the barn after milking the cows. Maggie had been helping her mother in the kitchen while Gladys and Kate were doing their school lessons at the big round table. Eddie sat on the floor building a house from small wooden blocks. Everybody was excited and trying to talk at once and trying hard to be heard. It was a warm happy scene.

"Gladys, you and Kate put away your lessons for now and set the table for dinner. Maggie, you can help me." said Mary. "Everybody must be hungry."

Eddie was asking questions faster than they could possibly be answered. He was a typical, inquisitive, five-year-old boy. John reached down, picked him up, gave him a big kiss on the cheek and put him on his shoulders.

"Look at me! Look at me!" Eddie demanded. Everyone laughed at him.

John gave his sisters and Eddie the remainder of the licorice sticks.

The guys stepped outside onto the open back porch. Like the front porch, it also ran the full width of the house. There were large galvanized wash tubs and a large galvanized boiler hanging from the wall.

Frank reached into his shirt pocket and pulled out a small leather pouch of tobacco and a curved pipe. He lit it with a wooden match that he had struck against a small rock.

The evening was warm with just a whiff of breeze coming through.

"It is peaceful and quiet here." Al remarked. "Tomorrow promises to be clear and sunny. We had lots of rain until about a week ago. We were keeping an eye on the Big Sioux."

"Need to take care of my horse, if that's all right?" John asked. Off to the left was a new barn and a tack room. John put Eddie on the horse and led the bay into the stall. Then John lifted him off the horse while he removed the saddle and bridle. Frank put down fresh straw while Al set a bucket of grain in front of the horse. While the horse ate, John rubbed him down.

"Stopped at the White's store in town. That's where I got the information to find you all. Do you know Jane White?" he asked Frank. "I'd like to get to know her better. Does she have a beau or is she spoken for? Don't want to get in anybody's way."

Reaching down, he picked up the gear and hung it on the wall close to the stall.

"We see her once in a while at the store. She had been here a few times with her folks." Frank answered. "Al got here about six months ago and I got here right after the fightin' was over. Neither one of us are interested that way. Haven't heard anything else."

Coming out of the barn, Tom started pointing things out to him as they walked towards the house. Next to the barn out of the weather, were two cast iron plows, a threshing machine, a couple hay rakes, and two large wagons. A large shed was being built to house the equipment and a two-seat buggy to carry the family. Meantime the buggy was being housed in the barn to keep the black shiny leather seats from being ruined by the weather.

Two large hog-pens with several sows and piglets, and a smaller pen with a boar in it, recently had been added to the area. Closer to the house was a large chicken coop with dozens of chicken running loose inside.

Off to the side of the house, about a hundred yards, was a bunk-house with a cook shed. "We got five hands and a cook. Even with the three of you here, we'll keep 'em on. Lots of work to be done and plenty for everyone to do."

Close by, ran a sizeable stream, fed by a fresh spring. A small spring house was built over it. This kept all perishable foods such as meats, milk, cream and butter, cold so they wouldn't spoil.

Closer to the house was the root cellar where the vegetables and fruits were kept.

Looking in the pasture and beyond the barn were several horses running loose and a herd of Holstein dairy cattle grazing on the grass. Tom had decided long ago that he would have a dairy farm. Mary made butter from some of the cream and used some of the buttermilk to cook with. Milk and cream that weren't used, were taken to town every morning along with most of the eggs that had been collected the day before.

Acres of corn, oats, soy beans, alfalfa, and other grains gave the flowing landscape the effect of a deep green carpet.

"We will show you the whole kit-n-kaboodle tomorrow, John", Tom broke in. "We will have lots of land to cover and things to see."

"Dinner is ready and will soon be on the table!" Maggie said, as she came out of the house and onto the porch. "Ma sent me to get you."

John grabbed the handle of the cast iron water pump and pumped water over his head, face, and arms. He was handed a towel, that had hung from a nail. "This is the life," he commented as he turned and put his arm around his sister and they went into the kitchen.

Everyone seated themselves around the big table. Eddie insisted that John put him on a stool and set it next to him. He wouldn't let John out of his sight.

Mary and Maggie served corn-on-the-cob, whipped potatoes and gravy. Tom sliced a large beef rump roast. Each dish was passed around the table to the left, while everyone helped themselves and filled their plates. A glass of cold milk sat at the right upper corner of each plate. The aroma of hot rolls filled the kitchen, mingling with the smell of apple pie.

After they had eaten, they thanked Maggie and Mary and complimented them on the great meal. Mary poured coffee and sat down. Tom got up and stood behind Mary's chair. Hitching his thumbs into his bib overalls, he looked over the table.

"This is the first time in many years that your Ma and me have had all of our family around. It's a wonderful feelin' and we've never been prouder or happier than we are right now. We are fortunate that our sons were returned to us." he said as he got his handkerchief from his back pocket and wiped his eyes.

"Do any of you have plans for your future?" Tom went on. "Your mother and me would like to have you boys throw in with us here. There's plenty of good land and we could use the help. When you're ready, each of you could build a house and have your own life. Figured we could all pitch in and help build it. Anyway, don't have to decide right now. Think about it and let us know. Your mother and me have talked this over many times and this is what we want to do. Oh! Hell! We've built all this up for all of us to have."

"Well! Thinkin' for myself, I don't need to think it over. I don't have any plans made. Can't think of anythin' I'd rather be doin' or any place that I'd rather be than right here. Count me in, Pa." Frank said.

"I was thinkin' the same as you, Al. Fact is I was thinkin' that this is real good country to put down some roots. Count me in too, Pa." John spoke up. "This is a real great idea."

"Me, too. Can't think of a better idea than this." Al offered. "Let's go outside and get some fresh air."

After shaking hands, hugs and pats on the back, the guys headed outside.

"Eddie jumped up from the table and headed for the back door following behind John.

Mary caught him by the collar and asked, "Where do you think you are goin? It's your bedtime!"

"I don't wanna go to bed! I wanna go see the big guys!" he said as he struggled to get out of his mother's grasp. "Sides, I wanna' show Missy and the puppies to John. He hasn't seen 'em yet." Eddie had a Collie dog that he named Missy and she had four new puppies.

"You can show them in the mornin'. Anyway it's too dark now. Why didn't you show 'em when you were in the barn earlier?"

"We didn't have nuf' time!"

Upstairs with you! I'll come up and tuck you in." Mary said, as she took a kerosene lamp from the side board and waited to follow him.

He gave everybody a big hug and after getting John's promise that he would see him in the morning, he slowly headed up the stairs, looking behind him to see if his mother had changed her mind. Seeing that she wasn't going to, he went on up to his room.

GOIN' TO TOWN

"I've been home for two weeks and it feels like I just got here. Every day has been different and each day is somethin' new to look forward to. It's a great feelin'!" John said at the breakfast table over pancakes, eggs, ham and coffee.

"Thought I'd ride into town, get a hair cut and see what's goin' on. The day I came, I kinda hurried here so I really didn't see much. Ma needs some needles and a few other thin's from the store. Told her I would get 'em for her. Will you be needin' me today, Pa?"

"You go ahead, son. You should have taken some time before now. Look around and explore. The town is a nice quiet place. It won't be long before it's a city.

People are startin' to come in. Go on and enjoy the day!"

"We know why you're goin' to town!" said Al. "It wouldn't be because of some little filly, now would it?" The guys started teasin' their brother good naturedly. "Want us to come along and introduce you? Pa will give us time off, too. Won't you, Pa?"

Before Tom could answer, John swung at Al with his fist good naturedly and Al ducked out of the way laughing. They all started laughing as John got up from the table and went out the door.

"See you later! I will probably be gone all day but I won't be very late. "John told them.

John went to the corral and caught the bay. He had turned him in with the other horses, into the pasture, the morning after he came. He brought him in last night so he could use him. John got him saddled and headed for town.

He noticed that things looked different from the first day that he had come through. He wasn't tired today nor was he in a hurry, so he could just take his time and see everything. He was really looking forward to seeing Jane and hoped that she was at the store.

'It was embarrassing the way the guys teased me. Maybe they're right.'

'I don't know what is the matter with me. I've known girls before. Is this the real thing? She is really cute and has such a pretty smile! Maybe she has been thinkin' of me. Why would she? There are several young guys around. Oh, well! I'll go and see her anyway," he argued with himself.

He rode on into town, bypassing the road that took him to the river. Maybe he would stop on his way home and see if the boys were around. He thought that they would probably be fishin' or doin' somethin' that boys that age liked to do.

When he was a kid, he liked to climb trees best of all and pretend that he was captain of a pirate ship out in the ocean. His mother was always telling him to stay out of the trees. She would always give him a stern talking to. He liked to go swimming in the old swimming hole, too. It was sheltered by a clump of large trees close to their childhood home.

Looking around him, he saw the stables with the blacksmith shingle hanging from a piece of iron above the opened double front doors. This was as good as time as any to meet the boy's father.

Walking up to the man with the large leather apron on, John shook his hand, "My name is John Taylor. The family lives north of town on the Big Sioux River. Maybe you've heard of 'em?"

"Yeah! I certainly have. I'm called 'Big Jake'. Guess you know why?" he said in a rolling jovial voice. The man stood six foot four inches tall and weighed around two hundred and fifty pounds with out any fat on him.

"The wife and I came down from Minnesota just after our boys were born. This has been a great place to live. The towns-people are friendly and neighborly. I consider myself as one lucky Swede!" Jake said.

"Have to keeping working. Promised a fellow I'd have his horse shod for him this afternoon. Don't mind, do you?"

John waited and watched as Jake shaped a horseshoe. Putting his big gloves back on and using large tongs, Jake heated a piece of iron over an open bed of hot coals until it was yellow and red hot. He held it, hitting it with a large sledge hammer against an anvil iron to shape it and once in a while dunking it in cold water. In this way he molded his horseshoe.

The water hitting the hot coals made small clouds. The steam rolled off his body. The work was hot and sweat trickled from his face and body.

"Heard that you came home to stay. It was mentioned over at the saloon and my boys' mentioned it, too. About all they could talk about around here for a couple days was meetin' you and fishin'. They keep tellin' me that I have to meet you. You are surely their hero! Guess they get into their share of trouble but nothing big. We are proud of 'em."

"Don't know about the hero stuff.! They are good kids! I found 'em along with 'Dog' on the river bank. They just kinda took me in." said John. "They like nothin' better than fishin'!" "We'd like to have 'em come and stay. Hope you and the wife can come visit, too. I know the folks would enjoy your company."

"I'm on my way to get a haircut and maybe a shave. I have to go to the store to pick up a few thin's for my mother. I just wanted to stop and meet you, introduce myself and say, hello. I'd best be goin' but I'll be seeing you soon." Tipping his hat, he got on his horse and rode on. Having a good feeling about Jake, he headed for the store.

Entering the store, he saw the same barrels and nothing had been changed that he could see. He spied Jane standing on a stool, stocking some canned goods by the counter.

"Hello! Good to see you agin'." he said. Startled, she turned around fast and caught her long skirt on a nail and started to fall from the stool. He quickly caught her before she could fall to the floor. "Are you all right? I am so sorry! I should have made some noise."

His heart was beating so fast he was sure that she could hear it. He helped her up and then quickly stepped back from her.

"It wasn't your fault !" said Jane. "That was silly of me. My mind was on what I was doin'. Thank you very much. Please! Give me a few minutes to compose myself."

Her heart was beating very fast, not so much from the near fall but from being so close to John. She had been thinking of him constantly and suddenly he just seemed to appear from nowhere. She knew that she was in love and hoped with all of her heart that he could feel that way, too. He always looked so calm and composed.

John thought that she was absolutely beautiful in her blue checkered cotton dress with the pretty little bows on the sleeves. Her hair was piled on the back of her head like the wings of angels. He knew that he had to see her again.

"I would like to see you agin'. Would your folks mind if I came around some evenin'? I would like to meet 'em, too." John managed to stammer as he was held mesmerized by her.

"That would really be nice." she managed to say. "I know they won't mind at all. They'd like to meet you, too. Pa just left a few minutes before you came in. You just missed him." "If you don't have plans, why don't you come for dinner tomorrow night. We usually eat at six o'clock."

'I hope this is okay with Ma and Pa, she fretted to herself. I know it will be. I've never done anything like this before. I know the folks will like him. He is such a wonderful guy!'

"I'll be there!" John knew that he had fallen in love.

"Oh! By the way! My mother needs a few thin's. Here is her list." He followed Jane around the store, helping her fill the order. He seemed to be walking on clouds. He didn't seem to notice anything around him until a customer walked up and asked Jane a question. John knew that he was in love. He knew that he had to see her again. He would make up excuses to come to town and the store.

FISHIN'

Coming to the road he had taken previously to the river, he decided to see if his young friends were there. Riding along, he found the same worn path. Getting off his horse, he walked to the river bank. Looking off to his right, just as though they hadn't moved, were Zac and Nick with 'Dog'.

"Where have you been? Thought you'd be here 'fore this. Almost give up on seein' ya' agin'!" Zac said. "Are you ready to do some fishin'?"

"I'll fish for a while, then I have to get back to the farm. I'm just headin' home from town." John answered.

"By the way, I went to the blacksmith shop while I was in town. Met your Pa! A real nice fellow! We talked mostly about you boys. Asked him if he'd mind if you came to visit us at the farm for a few days. Maybe some time soon. He thought it was a nice idea, if you want to. What do ya' think?"

The boys looked at each other and grinned a big wide grin.

"Really! Guess I'd like that better than anythin'!" Zac answered, hardly able to contain his excitement. "We don't go much. Pa works all the time except when we go to church on Sundays. What do ya' think, Nick?"

"I'm all for it! Lookin' forward to it!" Nick answered as he did a cartwheel. "Will it be anytime soon? Don't wait to long! I'm so excited that I have bubbles in my stomach and I wanna go now."

"This is real nice. I know that ya'll have a great time. There are lots of animals to see and lots of thin's to do. We have an ornery goose that loves to catch ya' when she can. She sneaks up behind and nips at your heels and behind. We have to keep a watch on her." John said.

"My brother Eddie is five years old." John went on. "He's a good boy but he can't sit still. My sisters, Maggie, Gladys and Kate are about your age. My brothers, Frank and Al are older than me. Do you have brothers and sisters?"

"No! Just us! Pa calls us his book ends. We are called twins because we look just alike. We are really different though when it comes to doin' stuff. I like to read and stuff. Nick doesn't!" Zac answered. Nick picked up a pole that he had made for John from a small limb. "Here you are." he said. "Been workin' on this since I saw you' last. It has a lot of give to it. Try it out! Throw in yer' line!"

Taking the pole and thanking Nick for his trouble, he oohed and aahed at the great feel it had in his hand. "What a nice pole. You did a great job and it really has a lot of play to it. You'll have to show me how to do this." John continued oohing and aahing over the pole as he cast his line in.

"Just figured that you'd need a fishin' pole and this way ya' could get right down to fishin'." Nick said. "But I will show you how to make one."

Making sure the pole was set, he settled down beside the boys and the dog on the warm grass and watched the blue skies. Once in a while a large billowy white cloud would show over their heads. They would try and guess at what it was shaped like. Sometimes it would resemble an animal and sometimes plants and objects.

"We've been wonderin' about the war. We hear thin's but just bits and pieces here and there. We talk about it but we don't know much." said Zac. "Hear ya' was in the war and yer brothers were too."

John explained, "Always remember that war is a very bad thin'. Many thousands of people were killed and families were ruined. Brothers fought and killed each other. Homes and properties were also destroyed. I don't want ya' to think it was a great thing to be in the war. Ya' didn't miss anythin'. Get comfortable, 'cause this is gonna take some time to tell." He went on.

The boys squirmed around as though to get more comfortable. Even 'Dog' moved around, laying down in the same place that he had been.

"Well! Everybody said that the reason the war started was to free the blackman. But that just wasn't so. The South wanted the manufacturing plants and the steel mills of the North and the North wanted the cotton, grains and resources of the South. The greedy owners got to talkin' and yellin' at each other and about each other until they had created mob scenes where ever they went. It wasn't long before it was spread over the country and the country was caught up in a tumult and war was started."

"Now ole Abe Lincoln got to be president and he was really against this war and destruction. He used the idea of slavery bein' abolished as a reason for the war. This means that we put a stop to the slavery. All of a sudden, this became the thought, reason and belief of what had caused the war. The industrialists were able to slide back into their place and continue as a united front. We're havin' a bad time tryin' to put thin's right agin' with the country. Nothin' will ever be the same as before."

"I caught somethin'." said Nick as he jumped up and grabbed his pole. There was a small fish dangling from it. "Just a small one but guess I'll keep it. Have you had a bite yet?"

"Not yet! Haven't even had a nibble." said John.

"Be quiet, Nick! So John can tell us more!" said Zac.

"Well. Abe himself, was a very smart man. Some people didn't like him 'cause of the slave situation. Others didn't like him 'cause he was endin' the war and there was a lot of greed goin' on. Not wantin' the war to end, they tried very hard to keep it goin'. Anyway, someone shot and killed Ole Abe one night while he was out at a theater with his wife."

"When the war started, my brothers, Frank and Al enlisted straight away. I was too young to join so I lied about my age and enlisted as soon as I could."

"Frank had been taken prisoner. He escaped and found his way back to his own outfit. He was made a sergeant. At a place called 'Shiloh', he was captured agin' and this time he was sent to the Andersonville Prison in Georgia. A place that wasn't fit for animals or humans."

"This was a terrible place. The prison consisted of only a few acres of land and was enclosed by high pinewood walls. It was a dirty mean place. The prisoners were starvin', some starved to death. There were too many prisoners for the space they had. They were mistreated, drank dirty water and didn't have proper food or medical supplies. This caused epidemics of scurvy and other bad diseases."

"What is 'pedmidics'? What happened to Frank?" Zac asked.

"Epidemics means everybody gets sick. Even little babies and great big people. Now don't interrupt me and I'll tell you all about Frank."

"Frank got with two fellows that came from the same general area where he had been fightin'. One of 'em had been wounded and was very sick. Now Frank knew that if he didn't get this guy outta there, that the guy would soon die and probably him and the other guy too. He started lookin' for a way to escape. He found a rotten place in the fence, where the fence wasn't put together quite right. He got his buddies to sit with their backs to it while he worked with rocks

39

and his fingers, workin' the rotten wood all day long until he made a big hole. That night, after dark, Frank worked hard makin' a big enough hole for the three of 'em to get through. They helped each other and made their escape. They carried and hauled their friend far back into the woods. Sleepin' in the day and keepin' a watch out, they moved at night in the dark. Stealin' food from the Rebs and usin' sticks to dig vegetables from long ago neglected gardens, kept the three of 'em from starvin', while they made their way back to their own lines. There was a lot of desertin' goin' on among the armies and Frank had a terrible time. He had been listed as missin' in action and the big army guys thought that he had gone over to the other side. He was cleared of all charges but in the meantime, he was kept in the guardhouse for a few days."

"Did he get any medals? Knew a guy that gotta medal for somethin' once." Zac spoke up.

"All three of the guys were very brave. Guess they all got medals. Frank got a special one and he got to be a lieutenant, too. He told me that he was scared the whole time."

"Hold it! I caught a big one this time! Can't hardly hold 'em! Help me! Wow! Look at how big he is! Must be around a pound and a half! Ain't he a dandy though? Whoopee!" John said.

The boys made a fuss over the fish. Letting John know that it was a special one.

"Well, you know I couldn't have caught it without this nice pole you made! I can't take him home with me. Not enough of 'em to go around. Will ya' do me a favor and take him off my hands?" John asked.

"Reckon, we'll just do that! Ma likes fresh trout. Pa doesn't get much chance to go fishin'. So we bring home the fish. Once in awhile, we catch a string of smaller ones. She likes that and she cooks 'em up. She is a great cook." said Nick. "Sure do thank ya'! Maybe we can catch some more."

"I really have to think about gettin' home. I have lazed around most of the day with you guys. It has been a lot of fun. I'm sure that my mother's waitin' for her thin's from the store. I will remember to let Ma and Pa know that I have asked you boys to visit and I will find out when is a good time."

JANE

John had been a nervous wreck since yesterday. His mind had been on tonight and his dinner with Jane and her family. His brothers hadn't been much help with their teasing. Al had offered to go along and drive the horse and buggy, and Frank had offered to go along and help Al. What great guys they are!

Ma had gotten out his old suit and pressed it for him. It still fit except the legs were a bit short. He would have Jane order some good wool for him and he'd make a new one. In the meantime this one would be okay. He hadn't grown that much since he had last worn it. He had shined his boots until they shone like mirrors. He was quite handsome in his bolo tie, suit, and new black hat.

Mary had told him how proud she was of him. She insisted that he looked just like his father.

She got a very thoughtful look on her face. "I remember when your father first came to dinner. It was just like yesterday. You look just like your father, John. Oh, well! Just reminiscing!"

"Go ahead and talk, Ma," John prompted. "I like to hear what went on before."

"Someday, John, we'll just set down and talk but for right now, we don't have the time. You have to get ready and get on your way."

He had hitched up the horse and buggy earlier and it waited in the front yard. It was ready to go when John climbed on and headed out. Mary had baked a cherry pie and sent it along for dessert. They had debated between apple and cherry. Mary had won, saying 'anyone can bake an apple pie.' She had wrapped it several times in flour sacks and it now rested under his seat. He would try not to hit the ruts.

As he rode along, he let his thoughts wander. Maybe Jane would be able to go for a ride. Can girls do that? He should have talked to Ma about these things.

Oh, well! He'd ask Jane and find out. He didn't want to do anything improper and end up embarrassing everyone.

Would the White's like him? He sure hoped that they would. Jane's brother John was a few years older than Jane and had been studying law. He would be a little bit older than John, maybe by a year. They sounded like a nice family.

Reaching the turn off to the White's, he drove between columns of large oak trees. Pulling up in front of a gray two story frame house, he noticed how pretty it was, nestled in a grove of big oak trees.

Just as he climbed out of the buggy, he heard someone ask his name. Turning around, he found himself face to face with an older man, a little taller than he was. "Hello! You must be John? William is my name, but everybody calls me 'Bill'. I'm Jane's father." He shook John's hand and put his arm around his shoulders.

"We have been lookin' forward to meetin' ya! Tie the reins around the rail there and come on in! How's Tom and Mary and the family? I keep thinkin' that Tom will be comin' into town and I'll be seein' him. I hear that he's real happy to have you guys home."

Opening the door, he let John go first. Standing just inside the door was Jane. His heart did a flip-flop! She was beautiful! She was wearing a pink satin dress with billowy sleeves and a vee neck inset of white satin. The ribbons in her hair matched the dress.

"Ma insisted that she send a cherry pie for dessert." As Bill went into the dining room, John handed him the pie. He was so easy to talk to that John immediately started to feel more relaxed.

"The family are excited about meetin' you!" Jane said as she led John into the parlor. "They have been teasin' me all day long. But they are wonderful."

"I know what you mean. Frank and Al offered to come along and drive the buggy."

At this, they both broke out laughing and the ice was broken. Bill came in and told them that Louise had dinner on the table.

Entering the dining room, John seen a guy about his age. Standing next to him was a young lady about Jane's age and an older woman that he presumed to be Jane's mother. A large oval table was sit formally with candle sticks and flowers on a lace table cloth. Everything was very homey.

"Family, this is John Taylor. I know ya'll know his family. John, this is my wife Louise! Our son John, but we call him Johnny and his fiancée, Catherine. She is our school ma'am." Bill made introductions, and John shook their hands and said that he was glad to meet them.

The men held the chairs for the ladies to sit down and then they sat down.

"I understand that you plan to stay on with your folks." Bill commented to John. "Tom told me, one time, that he hoped all of his sons would want to stay on the place. It's big enough."

The talk turned from John to the new bank in town. It was built of red brick and had a large gold printed sign announcing 'The Bank of Sioux City' with 'Proprietor J.R. Barnes', on it.

Mr. Barnes, a friendly, portly fellow came from the eastern part of the country. Some thought as far away as Maine but no one knew for sure.

Johnny was very excited about this. He had made a deal with Mr. Barnes to rent a corner space inside the front of the bank by the door, so he could have office space to start his law practice.

Bill had bought two lots next to the bank and had given them to Johnny for the purpose of building a law office. When he had his practice started, then he would start to build his office building. The town was growing and Johnny planned to grow with it.

With dinner over, Jane and Catherine sat on the veranda swing while John and Johnny sat in chairs facing them. They were discussing John and Catherine's wedding plans. Johnny was saying that as soon as his practice was well started that they would be married. Catherine didn't want to wait that long but she understood why.

John became thoughtful again. 'Would Jane marry me? She has to know how I feel about her. She has been looking at me all through dinner.. She has to have feelin's for me, too.'

He had to have a few minutes to talk to her about Rachael. She had to know about her. John had married

Rachael in Tennessee. She had gotten sick in child birth and died.

"Two weeks from Saturday night, they are having a 'Basket Social' at the school. John, do you think that you and Jane might want to go with us?" Johnny asked.

"What's a 'Basket Social'?" he asked.

"The women all fix a basket of food and halfway through the evenin', the baskets are auctioned off. Who ever gets that basket also eats supper with the lady that brought it. We are gonna' cheat! Catherine will do something special to her basket so I know which one to bid on. You and Jane could do the same thing. It's fun and the whole town turns out." Johnny explained.

"Would you like to go, Jane? It sounds like fun to me." John replied.

"Yes, I would really like to go. I've been hearin' about it at the store and the town is excited about it. Gives everybody a chance to get together and visit. Our folks are goin' and I'm sure that your folks will be there too." she answered.

Catherine and Jane started chatting about what they would wear and what they would fix for their baskets and the guys were chatting about other things. Soon the evening was over and it was time for John to leave for home and Johnny to take Catherine home.

They all went inside and said their thank you's. John made it a point to especially thank Louise for the wonderful dinner. He would be sure and tell his family that she had asked about them. He shook hands again with Bill and told everyone that he had had a very nice evening and thanked them for inviting him.

Jane walked with him onto the veranda. He reached down and kissed her lightly on the lips. He really wanted to take her into his arms.

"Can you sit a minute? I would like to talk to you about somethin' that is very important and I know that you really need to know."

"You look so urgent! My goodness! What is it?" Jane asked.

John started to explain, "Jane, I was married before in Tennessee. We moved to Blakesburg, Iowa. She died shortly after we were married."

Jane looked surprised. She interrupted, "Would you like to tell me about it? This must have been terrible for you."

"We met while I was in the army. I worked as a tailor, makin' special uniforms for the officers. She was the daughter of a major and would come with her father to get his uniforms and shirts fitted. We became friends and were married shortly before I mustered out of the army."

"She was carryin' my child and became very sick. The doctors couldn't do anything for her. Neither could be saved. She and the baby both passed away. They are buried in Wapello County Iowa. We had only been married for five months."

"After that, I just wandered around the country. My folks know and also Frank and Al. There hasn't been a need to tell anyone else until now. I have feelin's for you, Jane, and I want you to know. It isn't a big secret. Please tell your folks!"

Jane stood up and walked to where John was sitting. "You poor man! That was a horrendous thing that has happened to you. This is a part of your life that is very

51

sad. You know that I have feelin's for you, too. Your life has been yours until now. Thank you for tellin' me. I will tell my folks and I'm sure they'll feel the same about it as I do."

"Jane, it's gettin' late. Time for you to come in." her father said through the screen door.

"I'll be there in a few minutes." she answered.

She reached up, putting her arms around John, they kissed very passionately and said good night.

"I will see you very soon." he said as she slowly turned and went inside. 'What a wonderful lady!' he again thought. 'I do love her.'

He then turned toward the buggy and his ride home.

THE ENGAGEMENT

John, Frank and Al had ridden their horses to the school. They rode alongside the buggy where their folks and Maggie rode. Everybody was toasty and warm under their lap robes.

Tom had commented that he was thankful that they were early. This way he was able to put the horse and buggy close by the building out of the weather. It was proving to be an Indian summer but the nights were turning cool.

Arrangements were made earlier for Jane to come with Johnny and Catherine. They would meet up with John at the school. He went looking for them but they hadn't arrived yet.

He was very happy and had made very special plans and hoped all went well. He had ordered a set of wedding rings through Mr. Barnes at the bank, last week when he was in town. The rings had come in this morning. Tonight, he would be able to ask Jane to marry him and be able to give her the engagement ring. It was a gold band with a heart shaped diamond in the center. The wedding ring of smaller diamonds would nest around the larger diamond of the engagement ring when put together at the wedding.

Seeing the White's come in, he waited until they had made their way around the room, visiting as they went. He wanted to speak to Bill alone as soon as possible. He was getting more nervous by the minute.

He had a very tearful memorable hour at home with Tom and Mary. They had both been very pleased and very happy for John.

He said his hellos' as he walked up to the White's. "Bill, I have been waiting to talk to you! Could we step outside a minute?" John asked him. "I have something that I need to speak to you about."

They worked their way out the back door so they could have some privacy. The school was filling up with people and getting very noisy.

"Bill, I want to ask Jane to marry me! I love her with all of my heart. I think she feels the same as I do. I want to ask her tonight but I wanted your blessin' first. John said, nervously twirling his hat in his hands. "I talked to my folks before we came tonight. They are happy for us. We have their blessin's."

Walking closer to John, he shook his hand. "Jane's mother and I have felt this was goin' to happen. We both welcome you into the family and you have our blessing's as well. I'm sure that Jane will say, yes! We've been watchin' her and she has told us that she loves you."

"We are very happy about this." Putting his arm across John's shoulders, he gave him a big squeeze. "We have been worried that you haven't known each other very long. But seeing you tonight, I won't worry anymore about that. I'll tell Louise as soon as I get inside and I find her agin'."

They walked together back into the school, arm in arm. They both had big smiles on their faces.

Looking across the school room, John spied Jane, Johnny and Caroline come in the door. He found his way through the people. Taking Jane's hand, he looked around him and commented, "Look at all the people! I didn't think there were so many livin' around here. Look! There are our folks. Let's go say hello to 'em."

Turning to Johnny, he told him that they'd be back in a little bit. Taking Jane by the arm, John led her in the opposite direction from her folks. They walked right out the back door.

"Where are we goin'?" she asked, as she was pulled behind him.

Standing in almost the same spot as he had been earlier with Bill, he sat her down on the bench.

"Right here is okay." he said. "Jane, you have to know how I feel about you! I love you with all of my heart and I hope that you feel the same about me! Will you marry me?"

She threw her arms around his neck and kissed him long and hard. "I love you with all my heart. I thought

56

you couldn't help but know. I'm sure that everyone else does!"

Reaching into his pocket, he brought out a gold and white box. Taking off the lid, he took out the heart shaped engagement ring and slipped it onto her finger. He kissed her very lovingly.

Together they admired the wedding ring. He put it back into the box and promptly put it back into his pocket for safekeeping. She admired her engagement ring and told him how proud she felt and how much she loved him. They just held each other.

Jane's face was a reddish color. She was so happy. This and the beautiful silk emerald green dress she was wearing, made her absolutely gorgeous.

"We had better go back in and find the folks", Jane said. Her heart wanted to stay right there but she knew that they had to go back in.

Her father spied them coming in the door and led Louise to them. As though on cue, John's parents materialized also. They passed Jane along with big hugs. She showed her ring and everyone admired it.

Shaking John's hand and congratulating him, everyone wished him the best.

The band was playing when they came in but it stopped abruptly as Bill took over the stage.

"Tonight, young John Taylor here, asked for the hand of my daughter Jane, in marriage. She has accepted! We are very proud to welcome John into the family." He continued talking about joining not only friends and neighbors but also talked about having one big wonderful family.

"You sneaky old Fox! You sure caught us by surprise! Although watching you and Jane moon around lately, we should have known." With this, Johnny pushed John and Jane onto the dance floor. They were immediately joined by the parents and then everyone joined in.

The evening was going fast. It was now time to have the auctioning off of the supper baskets. Everyone stood around waiting for their baskets to be presented. Each one seemed to go quickly. Jane had told John to watch for a large red rose on the handle of her basket. He had bid $3.00 for it but was prepared to bid everything he owned.

John and Jane were soon sitting with Johnny and Catherine. Opening her basket, Jane took out plates, glasses and silverware. On these she arranged cold fried chicken, potato salad, coleslaw, pickles and large buns with butter.

For dessert were two large wedges of apple pie with slices of cheese on top. To round off the supper was a bottle of sparkling red wine that John had brought. They shared this with Johnny and Catherine.

"When is the wedding day?" Catherine asked. "Have you decided yet? What a thrilling surprise you have pulled off, John!"

"We really haven't talked about any plans or set any date." Jane answered. "I would like to get married in November. This will give us three months to get everything ready and we won't be rushed. I really don't want a long engagement. What do you think, John? Is this okay with you?"

John agreed by saying, "It is your day. You make the plans. Just keep me informed to what I am suppose to do or whatever you want me to do!" he laughed. He was so happy that he seemed to be walking on air!

The evening seemed to go by much to fast. The band quit playing and the evening came to a close.

Walking Jane to Bill's buggy, he told her that he would see her the next day. He gave her a big kiss and hug.

Jane went home with her parents, knowing that soon she would be married and have her own horse and buggy and going to her own home with her husband.

THE TAILOR SHOP

John and Jane hadn't had much time together so this afternoon they decided to go on a picnic. John had found a plush meadow with a creek running through it. They looked around and decided on a nice spot next to the creek where John immediately put the crock of lemonade to keep it cool.

Jane spread out a red and black checkered blanket. They then unloaded the buggy onto it. Jane had brought lots of food.

After they had eaten and things were cleared up, John laid back on the blanket. Taking her hand, he pulled her to him until she was laying next to him. He slowly put his arm under her neck and leaning over her, he kissed her with all the love he felt. She returned the kiss without holding back.

"I love you so much and I have since the day I first came to town. Remember the day that you fell into my arms? I thought that you could hear my heart beatin'. It was about to explode in my chest." John professed his love to her.

"I feel the same way John! I love you so much and I know that we will be very happy together."

"You are absolutely right." he chuckled.

Pulling himself up, he reached down and helped her to her feet. Holding her in a big bear hug, he kissed her.

"Let's go for a walk and see if we can see some more deer." Earlier a doe and fawn had been standing by the creek but they had disappeared into the trees.

John had been thinking about opening his own tailor shop and decided to bring up the subject. "How would you feel about me startin' up my own tailor shop? I have always thought that maybe someday I would. Maybe the time has come. I have saved up some money to get me started."

"I think it is a good idea." Jane answered as she took John by the hand and they both sat down on a large rock. "I've wondered if you were thinkin' that way. All the town's people would sure like it. Some send as far away as St. Louis to get their clothes. You would be handy for 'em."

Rubbing her shoe back and forth in the dirt, She looked at John and said, "I love to work making ladies hats. I have made several just for the ladies around town. They seem to think that I am quite good at it. Could I have part of your shop for millinery? We would make a good team, you and I."

"Wouldn't this be great?' he whispered in her ear. He took her in his arms and kissed her. "We will make a great team! We'll discuss this more later. Right now we had better get back and pack up the buggy. It looks like rain and we should be heading for home before we get wet."

He had run into the twins in town and they hadn't wasted any time letting him know that they felt like he was ignoring them. Zac had said, "Guess you don't have time for us now that you have a girlfriend!"

He hoped that he had been able to explain things to them. They would always be friends no matter what and they could come and see the him anytime they wanted, too. He asked them to be part of the wedding and they gave a big 'whoopee' and smiled their big smiles.

On different occasions, they had spent several days at the farm with John and his family. They all had great times and became lasting friends. One time, he had been in the barn milking when the boys, followed by Eddie, came in to play with Missy and the puppies.

"Come over here, Nick! Do you want to learn to milk a cow? Here, sit down on the stool," John said as he got the stool and made room for him. The cow mooed and moved a little bit, swishing it's tail. Nick panicked and jumped back, kicking the pail of milk over and spilling most of it.

"Are you all right?" John asked, as he helped Nick up. He was trying very hard not to laugh. The expression on his face was just too much and John burst out laughing and so did everyone else.

The fear was soon forgotten and John had let each of the boys milk for a while until they were tired of it and they decided to find something else to do.

John arrived at the White's home, where he seemed to spend a lot of his time, as Jane came out of the house onto the porch.

"Hello!" she said as she gave him a big hug. "Let's sit out here for a while. Ma and I have been cookin' and the house is hot and stuffy."

John took her hand as they sat down. The weather was very warm for this time of year but it would be turning cool soon.

"After we talked and I found out how you felt, I really have been busy thinkin' and I've decided to open my own tailor shop. This is really what I want to do and you can have room to make your hats and etc. Like you said, 'We can make it'. I'm sure the town's people will be behind us."

"I talked to Jeb Thompson about renting his old place. It's the big house that sits on the right hand side of the road, going into town. "It's a big house. We can work out of the living room and parlor, using

65

the downstairs bedroom for supplies. We will still have the kitchen and the upstairs for living space. We will be close in where people won't have trouble getting to us."

"What do think? Maybe this will work out until we have the money to build our own place."

"Oh, John! I'm so happy! I can hardly wait. You have been able to put our dream together." Jane said. "When will I be able to see the house. I would like to get inside and do what is needed to get our living quarters set up."

"I guess at anytime. I will get with Jeb tomorrow and settle the deal."

"One other thing we have to talk about is our weddin' trip. I'm sure you have been concerned about this." he said with a big smile. "The paddle boat, 'The Queen', comes through here every four days. What do you think we take it to Kansas City? We can shop and look for sewing machines and what ever we need to get started. We will need materials, notions, and machines. We can have a nice trip and go do whatever you like. We could see a play? Make it a combination trip."

She could hardly contain her excitement. "Yes! Yes! Yes! You have thought of everythin'."

Standing up, she grabbed John and he grabbed her around the waist and tickled her. They kissed each other hard and long. Looking out of one eye, he released her, realizing that they had an audience.

Louise had just come out of the house with large glasses of lemonade. "Thought this would taste good." she said as she set the glasses on the table and turned to go back inside. "I'll be right back with some cookies, fresh out of the oven."

After Louise went back into the house, John and Jane looked at each other and burst into laughter. They were very embarrassed.

Coming back, Louise set the cookies on the table next to the lemonade. "Come and join us, Louise." John invited her. "We have been makin' some plans for our future and weddin' trip."

Jane was so excited and happy telling her mother all their plans.

Louise smiled. "I am so happy for you both. When are you going to do all this? We have to have some dates to go by. There is a lot of work to be done. The weddin', the house, and the trip."

"Jane, let me know what you decide for dates, so I can get arrangements made. Don't wait to long. Everythin' takes time." He picked up his glass and took a big drink.

"I have to be leavin' now. I promised Pa that I would help him this afternoon. I have to tell him our plans, too."

"Don't let me rush you off, John. I'll be going inside shortly. I have a lot of work to do in the kitchen." Louise said.

"I really do have to be going. Pa will be wonderin' where I am and if I'm goin' to be there. He gets a little nervous now and then." Getting up, he grabbed his hat. "I will let my folks know all that is goin' on."

John gave Jane a big hug. He then got on his horse and rode for home.

"When are you and Jane gonna decide where to build your house?" Tom asked as he and John were in the barn doctoring a cow that had stepped into a rabbit hole. "We had better get busy on it or it will never be finished in time for the weddin'! You don't have much time as it is."

"I've been meanin' to talk to you about this but I just never found the right time. Jane and I have talked and we have decided to rent the Thompson house on the edge of town for a while. It's not that we don't appreciate you and Ma. We do!" John answered.

"What has brought this on? I thought we'd be buildin' a house. Frank and Al are ready to start buildin'. You really need to explain what is goin' on. Why the change in plans?"

Seeing the hurt look on his father's face, John began telling his father what he and Jane had talked about. "Pa, I want to start a tailor shop and Jane wants to make hats for the ladies. The town is growin' up real fast. The people have to send for most of their suits, hats and bigger things. Sometimes it takes weeks to get things shipped in. This will make it easier for the townspeople and it's somethin' that we really want to do."

"We are goin' to Kansas City for our weddin' trip. While we are there, we will look around for equipment and supplies."

He went on to apologize, "We are so sorry, Pa. This was only decided for sure, today. I will get with Frank and Al and try to make things right with them. You are a wonderful bunch of guys. I wouldn't hurt any of you, without a good reason. You know this. Please understand and say it's okay!"

Tom was surprised. He was hurt but he wanted the best for John and Jane. "Of course it's okay with us. Anything we can do, you just let us know. I'm sure I'm speakin' for all of us. I will leave it up to you to tell your mother and the rest of the family. They will want to know right away."

"If you need some money to help you get started, just let me know." said Tom. He stood up and gave John a big hug to let him know that all was well and that there weren't any hard feelings.

"I have some money put away, but if I need some I will certainly borrow some from you. Thanks, Pa!" said John.

Walking to the house, John felt torn between staying with the laid-back life of the farm and going with the unknown tailor shop. They had made their decision and would keep to it. If things didn't work out, they could always come back home and build a house. He would be a farmer like his father wanted him to be.

Tomorrow he would talk to Jeb and get things started.

THE WEDDING

Everything was happening fast. Several last minute touches had been done to the church by the church ladies. Mothers of the school children had gotten together and finished last minute touches to the schoolroom where the reception would be held immediately following the wedding. All the desks and other furniture had been removed.

Jane's beautiful white satin wedding gown with matching train and large bustle, hung in her bedroom. Hanging next to it was a beautiful white veil with petite white roses across the band. A large picturesque white satin hat with white streams down the back, a pair of elbow length white gloves and a pair of matching button-up shoes finished the ensemble.

Food had been prepared at the White's with the help of several of the town's ladies. Bill barbequed the hindquarters of a beef and Tom, not to be out done, had barbequed a full pig. Several of the town's women would set everything up. Catherine had asked the older girls in her classes to serve the guests when they arrived.

Everyone in town had been invited. It was impossible to leave anyone out without causing hard feelings. Between John and Jane, they seemed to know everyone. It was a special day for the town. A day that would always be remembered.

They had packed a buggy with valises and suitcases, along with all the things they were taking on their trip. Johnny had brought it to the church earlier. They would only have two hours for the reception and to change clothes and board the paddle boat.

The little country church was decorated with fall flowers: purple crocuses, purple hydrangeas, yellow asters, and purple and yellow mums. Each bouquet was wrapped with large white satin ribbons.

Nick and Zac ushered everyone to their seats. Tom and Mary Taylor sat in the front pew on the left side of the church while Bill and Louise White sat in the front pew on the right side. Soon the church was filled, overflowing into the churchyard. The excitement was filling the air.

The organist started playing the wedding march. John and Johnny came from the back room and met the Reverend Jones at the altar. Nick and Zac came forward and stood beside Johnny. They looked so fresh and handsome with their hair combed and in their black suits, white shirts and shining boots.

Catherine, Maggie and Gladys, the bridesmaids, came down the aisle in their pretty lavender taffeta dresses and matching large brimmed hats. They were slowly walking down the aisle, keeping time to the music. They were pretty girls but in their outfits, they were lovely.

John watched as Bill, with Jane on his arm, moved slowly towards him. He couldn't believe that she was really his. His heart felt like it was going to burst inside of him. She was a vision in white. The beautiful dress clung to her bosom and fell in large gathers from her waist. The small pearls around her neck were given to her by her father. She seemed to float on air.

The Reverend Jones, facing the people, said a wedding prayer. Johnny handed John the wedding ring and stepped back. The vows were exchanged as John placed the ring on Jane's finger. The Reverend then pronounced them husband and wife and told John that he could kiss the bride. John lifted the veil from Jane's face and kissed her deeply. There were tears in their eyes. They were very happy and very much in love.

Entering the school, they were met by a photographer. He had set up his tintype camera. He took several pictures of the bride and groom, bridesmaids and parents. A group picture was taken of the wedding party.

They continued into the school, hugging and shaking hands with everyone as they made their way towards the front of the room. The bridesmaids were waiting for Jane.

"I'll help here, arrange packages and get them ready to be opened." said Gladys as Jane was whisked away.

Laughing and chattering, Catherine and Maggie each took one of Jane's arms and hurried her to the small storeroom at the back of the school which they had pre-arranged to use as a dressing room. They helped her change from the beautiful gown into a gorgeous yellow traveling suit with matching shoes and parasol.

"We had better hurry into the reception. I'll pack up your weddin' gown and send it home with your mother." said Catherine as she hurried Jane along. "John will be patiently waitin' for you. We had better hurry."

A table was set up in the center with punch and glasses. In the middle of the table was a beautiful three-tiered wedding cake decorated with small candied green leaves and red roses. The table to the left was covered with beautifully wrapped packages and the table on the right was set up with every sort of hot dish, salad and food.

As the packages were opened, Gladys wrote down all the gifts and who sent them. They received pretty homemade quilts, a feather mattress and other bedding plus dish towels and pot holders. They also received dishes, pictures and about all things that a young couple needed to start housekeeping.

"Come over here!" Catherine said as she started edging the newlyweds toward the cake. "You need to cut the cake. Here's the knife." She handed the knife to John.

"John! Look at me." Jane said. She put a small bite of cake into his mouth. They fed each other cake, laughing all the while.

The band played and the newlyweds led everyone in the first dance and reveled in the festivities. It was a wonderful time but time was getting short and they knew they had to hurry to the 'Queen'.

All the single girls gathered in a group. Turning her back to them, Jane threw her bouquet over her shoulder. Catherine stepped forward and caught it. Everyone was laughing and teasing her. It wouldn't be long before she and Johnny were married. His law business was starting to grow, so hopefully it wouldn't be much longer.

Johnny had gone ahead to the boat. Unloading the buggy, he carried the baggage into their stateroom so everything was ready for them when they got there. He had left a large basket of fruit and a bottle of champagne for their trip.

They would be in Kansas City in the morning!

KANSAS CITY

Walking from their stateroom toward the casino, Jane noticed the snowflakes coming onto the deck. "This is a wonderful trip. I'm glad we have taken it. The weather is perfect for this time of year!" she said as she and John wandered out onto the deck of the 'Queen.' "I am so happy! No one could be happier! John, do you feel this way too?"

Stopping her, he took her into his arms and kissed her. "Jane, my life changed when I met you. I am every bit as happy as you are and I'm lookin' forward to the rest of my life with you."

The loud music and the voices of the casino, put them into a partying mood and they joined the crowd.

They wandered to the cashier's cage, where John bought chips, then they went on to the roulette table.

John placed a five dollar chip on #5 red. The ball went around and around on the wheel stopping on #3 black. He put another five dollar chip on #5 red. Again the ball went around and around on the wheel stopping on #5 red. "This is fun!" he said. He gave Jane some chips so she could try her luck.

Jane had never seen gambling before although she had heard the guys talk about it when they came into the store. Mostly they talked about the poker games at the saloons. She placed a dollar chip on # 3 black and #7 red came up. She played several times and finally her numbers came up. This was all new and exciting to her.

They walked around sampling the different types of games. As the evening wore on, they decided to cash in their chips and call it an evening.

The river seemed very calm and the boat traveled along as though the river was standing still. Their stateroom was large and roomy.

They would be disembarking soon and they were looking forward to exploring Kansas City. Meanwhile they had everything packed and they were ready to leave the boat as soon as they were given the okay.

They had spent hours going over their list of supplies and machines that they would be shopping for. They had a long day and a lot of work ahead of them.

First they just wanted to get checked into their hotel room, and then have something to eat. The day was all theirs!

"All ashore! All ashore!" said the captain's mate. They walked down the gangplank onto the shore being carried along with the crowd.

"Don't get separated from me!" John told her. "In this crowd, I would never find you again! Here grab my arm and hang on tight!"

"I'll rent a horse and buggy to take us and our things to the hotel."

Just at that time, a lone man with a horse and buggy came up to john. He had a sign on the buggy that read 'FOR HIRE'.

"Do you need help, sir?" the man asked.

Stepping forward, John answered. "Yes. We do! Will you take us and our things to the Cattleman's Hotel?"

They were having a hard time keeping upright. The ground was partially frozen and the snow sloshed under their feet. Suddenly Jane started slipping and grabbed for John's arm but missed him. She lay sprawled in the snow. They were laughing so hard that she couldn't get up and when John reached down to get her hand, he fell too. They lay laughing until the man helped them up. Soon they had the buggy loaded and were on their way.

Riding along was almost like being in another world. The horses and buggies, the beautifully dressed ladies in their gorgeous clothes and striking hats, and the gentlemen in their fancy suits, vests and hats were everywhere.

"Lookin' at the people, I can hardly wait to get everythin' put together and start our business." John said. "Have you seen how advanced the styles are here compared to Sioux City?"

"I have been lost in the people and the scenery! Everythin' to me is absolutely overwhelmin'." Jane replied.

"After we freshen up and have somethin' to eat, we can go explorin' the city, if you want to? I think it would be interestin'." he commented. "We have reservations for dinner at six and the stage show afterwards. But I'm sure we have time to see some of the City."

"The name of the show is 'Chicago Revue', a musical. I have never been to one before." she told him. "Have you? I understand that the show comes all the way from Chicago."

It will be somethin' to remember." he said.

The hotel was a three story structure of large special cut sandstone squares. It had two hundred rooms in which to accommodate the guests. A large dining room with a large stage area, held the most recent stage acts from Chicago. There was also a band and dance floor.

John carried Jane over the threshold. Entering their room, They were pleasantly surprised. It was furnished with a large French double bed, covered with a goose feather comforter. A large matching wardrobe hugged the far wall. A ewer of water and a basin sat on a matching commode under the window in the center of the room. The window had been raised several inches to let the fresh air in. It was covered with bellowing white sheer curtains. Persian scatter rugs were placed around the floor and in front of the bed.

John helped Jane take off her jacket and removed his own. Walking to the window he drew the curtains aside and looked down on the street and the people. What a bustling sight!

They immediately started putting things into the wardrobe. Jane teasingly threw small items of clothing at him and soon they were laughing, hugging and kissing. They were thrilled with each other and everything they did together was great.

John and Jane entered the dining room and noticed small tables set for two, others set for four and larger tables had been set up to accommodate parties of six and larger, depending on the size of the dinner party.

They were shown to a table by the window by a young waiter dressed in black pants, white shirt and a black bow tie. Helping Jane with her chair, he said "Ill be right back with water and take your order."

Looking out the window, the crowds of people seemed to be everywhere. Children with their parents, storekeepers, ranchers and cowboys, all types of people from all corners of the country seemed to meet here. The way the people dressed was a testament to their way of life, each group, a story of their own.

The waiter returned to take their dinner order. John ordered the sirloin steak, fried potatoes, green beans and coffee with chocolate cake for dessert, ordering for them both.

"I'm very hungry and ready to eat." Jane remarked. "It is nice to just relax and watch the people. It is fun to just watch. I'm getting great ideas from the ladies' latest millinery fashions."

After they had eaten, the waiter removing all the dishes and clearing the table, said "We are gettin' ready to start our show. You have a good table and will be able to see everything."

The music started and the curtain was raised. The dancing girls entered the stage, dancing into the arms of the male dancers, as they danced from the other side of the stage. During the evening, they sang and did dancing routines and comedy acts. The bright costumes and lively music made a wonderful evening. It was almost magical. It soon ended and the evening was over.

SHOPPIN'

Jane stretched several times and threw her arm over the bed to where she thought John was. Feeling around the spot, finding him not there, she panicked. Where was he and why hadn't he awakened her. Jumping out of bed, she threw on her heavy robe.

The door opened and John came in. "Good morning, honey! You were really sleepin' sound and I didn't want to wake you up. Thought I would run down to the kitchen and get us a cup of hot coffee to drink while we are gettin' dressed. We can go later for breakfast and then go shoppin', if you want."

Setting the cups of coffee on the commode next to the ewer, he put his arms around her and gave her a big kiss. "I'm sorry! I didn't think you would be awake until I returned." he apologized.

"I was just worried. I woke up and you weren't there. Thank you! The coffee is great and you know that I'm excited about shoppin'. Let's hurry and get goin'."

They entered 'Wilson's', a large fabric and sewing machine shop. "Can I help you?" asked a clerk as he came up to them.

John explained what they were lookin' for. Following the clerk towards the back of the building, they came to several sewing machines with different brand names.

He spotted a Glover & Baker brand machine, made of cast iron and encased in a walnut cabinet. He checked out the wheels, cables and pedals to be sure that everything was okay and not to complicated. He then checked the tension and bobbins. Sitting down, he threaded the bobbin and placed it into the machine. He then threaded the machine. Using a thick piece of wool cloth, he made a seam to be sure that the stitches were smooth and even.

"I'll take this machine." John told the clerk. I also spotted a Florence brand. It is smaller and will work much better for you, Jane."

He sat down and went through the machine as he had earlier. Everything again checked out. He had Jane try the machine. She really liked it, so John told the clerk that they would take this one too. Both machines were built for all thickness of material.

Now that the machines were set aside, they went on to the materials. Jane picked out pieces of lace, ribbons, furs, wools, feathers, hat pins and buttons. John picked out bolts of muslin, cottons, ginghams, linens, silks, wools and netting. He bought large spools of thread of different colors and weights. He bought several pair of scissors, small and large, measuring tapes, needles, pins, hooks & eyes and all notions they might need.

He ordered two dress forms, two tailor suit forms, and four hat blocks.

It took the better part of the day to check everything out. Some things had to be ordered in from Chicago. By the time that John had paid for the merchandise and told the clerk that they would be returning in the morning, the sun had gone and it was starting to snow. What a beautiful day!

Waking early after a very restless night, John got out of bed and was watching out the window at the falling snow. Kansas City had gotten into his blood. He had been thinking that he would like to move here and set up his shop. Jane seemed to like it here too.

"Good mornin' sleepyhead." he said as he tweaked her nose. She moved her head and brushed her nose as though she was swatting a fly. Opening her eyes, she grinned at John.

"You are an early bird!" she said. "What! No coffee! I am gettin' spoiled already."

"I didn't want to leave you, after scarin' you yesterday mornin'. Maybe we should go down to breakfast and have our coffee."

"I really am in love with Kansas City. It has really gotten to me. I don't know just what it is or if it is just everything. The hustle and the people. It is so alive!"

She started to speak but he hushed her by saying "Please hear me through on this and then I want you to tell me what you think."

"I've been awake most of the night thinkin' about this. I watched you yesterday and I got the idea that you feel about the same as I do. Guess that what I'm trying to say is that I would like to move to Kansas City and start our business here."

"It will mean leavin' the families but we aren't that far away and we could visit back and forth as often as you would like. Our folks will have a lot to say about it but I think they'll come around to our way of thinkin'."

"Oh John! I thought 'What If' all day yesterday. What if we had our shop here, we could. Can we really move here? We wouldn't have to ship our supplies. I think that 'Wilson's' store will hold our things until we find a place and we can get moved and set-up."

"You are so wonderful. You are always thinkin' and full of ideas. I just know we won't have any problems.

Hugging each other, they sealed their futures. They got dressed, went downstairs to breakfast and then on to 'Wilson's store'.

OUTLAWS

The reconstruction of the south despite the good intentions of the government was a terrible nightmare for all concerned.

The government sent men from the Freedom Bureau and other reconstruction agencies to the south. These men were soon known as carpetbaggers. Everything they owned, they carried in carpetbags. Most of these men went only for their own greed. They controlled the vote of the black man and set up a dishonest government. Rather than help the people to work together to reconstruct the south, they stole everything for themselves. They soon joined with their southern counterparts known as scalawags. Both groups were hated and resented by the southern people. They took over the lands, homes and properties and then killed the owners or ran them off.

Other riffraff came from the north looking to get what they could for nothing. There didn't seem to be any control over these people. They did what they wanted.

The southern people that had lost their homes and means of existence fled north looking for work and a new life. They worked their way north through Tennessee into Missouri, Kansas, Iowa, Nebraska, and states farther north. When many couldn't find work, they turned to crime. The worst of the riffraff from the north and south seemed to congregate in the Kansas-Missouri area.

Outlaw gangs, gun slingers and lawless groups seemed to be haunting the area. The Dalton's, James Boys, Younger's, Earps and Belle Starr were a few of the well know gangs and Doc Holiday, Bill Doolin, Bill Hickock and Bill Cody were among the well known gun slingers.

Trains, stage coaches and banks were being held up and robbed. People were being killed. Cattle were stampeded and rustled. It was a lawless land and the people were at the mercy of the gangs and the lawless.

Men, who had put their guns away after the war, now took to wearing them where ever they went. They strapped them on every morning and took them off every night. They were never very far away from them. They wore them for the protection of their families and property. No one was safe. The easy life as they knew it was gone.

Jessie and Frank James with their neighbors, Cole, Bob and Jim Younger and their friend Charlie Pratt were in the Kansas City area hiding out from the law. They were staying with friends on a farm just outside of town. They were being hunted from Florida to North Carolina, to Kansas and as far north as Minnesota.

About everyday, Frank or one of the Youngers would ride into town to check and see if there was anything new happening.

Kansas City had just opened up a new bank. Frank James had been loitering around the outside. He had made this an everything to do. One day a messenger came to the bank and Frank followed him inside where the messenger went directly to the bank president. He got close enough to hear them talking. Frank learned that all the taxes had been collected and that they came to over $40,000. The money was being held in this bank and that an armed guard would come and collect the monies the next day.

Frank went to Jesse and they decided that the money should be theirs. They immediately started making plans to rob the bank and make their get away.

The next day, Jesse took a $100. bill to the bank and asked the cashier to break it down for him. The cashier had to go into the back room of the bank to do this. Using this as an excuse, he followed him into the back and tied him up. Then he opened the back door and let the gang in. They filled cotton bags with the money and leaving the cashier tied up and unharmed, they ran from the bank, got on their horses and headed out of town.

Someone from the bank fired two shots in the air to get the town's attention.

John and Jane were working in their shop when they heard the shots. He grabbed her and pushed her to the floor as he made his way to the front door and locked it. He looked out of the window but everyone had fled for cover leaving the street completely empty.

Suddenly some one banged hard on the door. "John, are you there? The bank has been robbed. We are formin' up a posse so we can get after them right away." The deputy said, "We need every man we can get. Meet us at the sheriff's office!" He continued on his way raising the alarm.

John didn't hesitate. Turning to Jane, he took her in his arms and told her, "I have to go. You know that I do. I'll be careful. It won't take long before we have them arrested and we'll be home again."

"I know you have to go." She had a shocked disbelieving look on her face. "Be very careful. I am too young to be a widow. Don't do anything foolish."

Releasing her, he grabbed his gun from a peg where he kept it hanging close, and strapped it on his waist. Leaving the shop, he headed for the barn and corral in the back. Catching his horse, he soon had him saddled and was headed for the sheriff's office where he met up with several of the men from town.

"We do know that Jesse and Frank James were recognized along with the Younger boys." the sheriff said as he swore each man in as a deputy. "This comes as a surprise to us. We didn't have a warning that they were even in the area. Be real careful, men. They are killers and they don't need an excuse to use their guns."

The men got on their horses and the posse followed the sheriff out of town towards the rolling hills, trees and cave complexes. They followed the route that they thought the outlaws had taken.

Stopping at a small ranch, the sheriff asked the rancher, "Have you seen anyone around here? The bank in town was robbed and we believe the outlaws are headed this direction."

"Are you sure they headed this way? There hasn't been anyone around this way for days except me and my crew. I'll ask around and see if anyone has seen any strangers or anything suspicious." The rancher swore that no one had been around.

They continued on into the brush, and cautiously into the cave area. Coming around a large clump of rock overlooking the river, they heard a horse whinny below them. The sheriff held up his hand to stop the men. They heard running horses as the gang made a run for it. When the posse got to the spot where the gang had been, they seemed to have vanished into thin air.

The posse scoured the rocks but came up empty handed. They knew that the gang wasn't able to get out without being seen from their direction. As quietly as they could, they inched their way toward the caves. They were sure that they were still there but well hidden or they had a secret way in and out of the cave complex. Keeping themselves hidden from the opening of the caves, they listened for the whiney of a horse or some noise that would give the gang away.

Satisfied that the gang had fled, and remembering the rancher, the sheriff decided to check out the ranch one more time. When they arrived, there didn't seem to be anybody around. No one answered the door. Something wasn't quite right. He decided to come back the next morning with his men and check everything out. Night had set in and the men were hungry and tired.

Just as he turned the posse towards home, he heard noise coming from behind the house. The posse took cover behind their horses and wherever they could. Nothing more happened but the posse stayed put for fear of being shot. They stayed where they were over night.

At first light, they started moving closer to the house. Part of the posse worked their way to the back while the sheriff and the others worked closer to the front. The sheriff yelled, "Give yourselves up, now! We don't want to shoot anybody, but we will. Don't make it hard on yourselves!"

Giving the gang ample time to answer, the sheriff then kicked the door open but nothing happened. Hurrying inside, he found an empty house. Only cans, garbage and such showed that the outlaws had been hold up there. They had slipped away during the night.

Hopefully someone would know or hear something and tell the sheriff. Until something came up, they had nothing to go on. The gang seemed to have gotten away. It was thought that they had a hideout somewhere in the caves and no one seemed to know who was living on the ranch. Everyone thought that the ranch house was not being used. The sheriff had been duped.

The town's people were panicked. They put up a $1,000 reward on the head of each gang member plus a $5,000 reward on the head of Jesse James.

Nothing more seemed to come out of it. The town seemed to settle down into a regular routine. They continued to watch over their shoulders and to check out all strangers that came to town but the town soon returned to normal.

The governor sent a U.S. Marshall from Topeka, but he wasn't able to do any more than the sheriff or the posse had done. He stayed around town and checked out the surrounding areas. He checked out the little ranch house but nobody seemed to be there.

TOMMY

John was pacing a hole in the floor of their living room. He had been pacing for hours stopping long enough to have a cup of coffee and sit with Jane.

This was his first child and he was nervous. Irene, the black midwife had been at this kind of work for many years and Dr. Johns had been in practice for forty years or more. Jane was in good hands.

Her parents along with John's parents had come from Sioux City on the paddle boat the 'Queen' to be here when their first grandchild was born. Because of the good natured bantering between the fathers, one would not come without the other.

Tom and Bill followed John outside to get some fresh air and light up their pipes. Time was drawing near and the tension was growing high. John was a nervous wreck. He couldn't help but remember his first wife, Rachel and their child that he had lost in child birth. He was scared that this could happen again, although it was very unlikely.

Mary came out onto the veranda, "Louise and I have fixed breakfast. When you are ready to eat something, it's there and you really need to eat something, and keep your strength up, son. Every thing is going to be all right. She is in very good hands. It won't be long now."

"Let's go in for breakfast while everything is still warm. Thank you Ma and Louise!" John said as he hugged them both. "I can't eat much but I'll try. I'm really not very hungry."

"I've been through having a baby seven times and each time was different. Always seemed to be the first time." Tom bragged as they sat down to breakfast. "I was just as proud and happy the seventh time as I was the first time."

A very loud baby cry split the air. Everyone stopped what they were doing and John jumped up and ran upstairs to the bedroom.

Irene met him at the door and wouldn't let him in. "You gotta' wonderful healthy little boy and our little mother's fine too. Maybe a little tired. Wait in the hall til' the Dr.'s done 'xaminin' him and I have prettied the little mama up."

John went downstairs to tell the folks. "We have a wonderful little boy." he said as his chest swelled out with pride. Looking toward the older men, he said "We have named him after you guys. Figured you'd like that."

"We can all go up in a little while." he said.

It wasn't long before Irene called them back up to the bedroom.

"You go on, John. We'll be up in a couple minutes. You need some time to be with Jane and the boy." Bill told him as he and Tom stayed seated. They began bantering back and forth about the baby.

"Guess I won that bet. You owe me five dollars, Bill." Tom laughingly patted Bill on his shoulder. "It always seems nice to have a boy come first. Kinda head of the family and protective sort of thing. A pretty sassy little girl would have been okay too. Maybe next time!"

"I sure don't mind losin' this bet. It is good to have a boy first ," Bill mused " but all of us would have loved a little girl just as well."

"Know what you mean. Us too." Tom put in. "Kinda miss having a little one around. It has been a few years."

John entered the bedroom where Jane was in bed. She had on a clean white night gown and her long hair had been combed and pushed back from her face with combs. Laying beside her was a pink faced, beautiful baby boy. Leaning over, he hugged them both and gave each a kiss on the cheek. He felt so proud; he thought his chest would explode.

Lifting the baby gently into her arms, Jane handed him to his father. "Here you go, Tommy. Go see your daddy." she said to the baby.

John was very awkward and he felt afraid he would drop him. He held him close to his chest. He had never held a new born before.

"He's not made outta glass and he's not a gonna break." Irene told him with a big toothy smile. "Whatcha namin' him?"

"We are namin' him after his grandpa's. His name is 'William Thomas." Jane answered. "April 18th, 1873 at 8:25 in the morning. What a great day!"

"What a legacy for him." John laughed pointing towards the door "Tryin' to keep up with them two! He'll always have his hands full. But two greater grandpas' he couldn't find. They are great guys."

Turning to John, she beamed "It's a miracle! I'm so glad that all has gone well and he's so perfect. He looks like you. Don't you think so?"

Before John could answer, Dr. Johns came over to them. "You have a healthy, happy baby. I know that you will be a nice little happy family." he commented. "I'll be leavin' now but I'll be back in a few days to check-up on the baby and see that all is well with mama." he smiled at Jane.

The grandparents came in. Bill and Tom were discussing who the baby looked like the most, the Taylor's or the White's? Of course, Tom was sure that he was the image of John.

Leaving the grandpa's to debate the issue, he walked outside with the Doctor to his rig. John thanked him again and pressed some money into the palm of his hand as they shook hands.

"Well, Daddy, how does it feel?" he said to the new father. "The newness and the shock will wear off and everythin' will become routine. These little guys really get under your skin. Sometimes you really wonder who's the boss. I know you will be great parents. So with that I'll leave you but I'll be back in a few days to see how things are goin'." He climbed into the buggy and drove away.

Jane had been kept busy with the house, shop and Tommy. Suddenly he was two years old and was a hand full. He was very active and talked up a storm.

She missed going and visiting her friends in the outlying areas. Most of the people were poor and had little to live on. She would fix baskets of food and take to the women. Now she would take the clothing that Tommy had outgrown and hopefully someone could use them for their children.

"I plan another visit in a few days with my friends. Tommy is old enough now to go with me and they keep askin' me when I will be bringin' him. They would like to see him." she said to John one day when they were relaxing after a long day in the shop. "I won't have to leave him with you anymore. He will have a great time with all the other little kids."

"I need to see Karry Martin. She is so interestin' to talk to and she is goin' to show me how to make bread from a recipe she brought from Scotland. She drops into the shop every now and then. You remember her, don't you?"

About this time they heard a loud crash. Both jumped up and ran into the kitchen just in time to rescue the dishes from falling on Tommy's head. He was attempting to climb to the top of the cupboard.

He clapped his hands together and laughed when he saw that he had an audience. He was a very inquisitive all American boy. He certainly kept mama and daddy busy.

"You need to sit on a chair for awhile so you can think about what you just did. You could have gotten hurt really bad." John admonished him. "What if that cupboard would have fallin' over on you? We wouldn't have a little boy anymore."

Jane put the food baskets and clothing into the buggy. She had brought extra food for Tommy and things for him to snack on during the day. She told John goodbye and Tommy reached up and hugged his daddy.

"We will see you in a while, Daddy." he said. "I'm gonna go with Mama so I can be her helper today."

They got into the buggy and slowly drove out of town with Tommy asking questions all the while.

Entering the Martin's yard, Jane and Tommy were met by several children and three dogs. Karry Martin came out of the house, wiping her hands on a dishtowel as she waved and welcomed her friend. She told the older children to help Jane unload the buggy. It wasn't long before the buggy was empty and the children were oohing and aahing over Tommy.

"Can we take him outside?" one of the older girls asked. "We will watch him close."

"That would be nice. He is a real handful and very mischievous. He will wear you out in no time." Jane smiled at her as the kids all ran out of the house and down the stairs.

Karry poured coffee and sliced a sweet nut bread to go with it. They were going through the things that Jane had brought when the door flew open and Nancy the oldest barged in, the blood drained from her face. She yelled, "Come quick! Tommy's been bit by a snake."

"We were pickin' up rocks and seen the snakes. Tommy reached for one and we pulled him back and told him no. Tommy grabbed for one anyways. He was to fast for me. The snake struck and bit him on the arm." Nancy explained hysterically, while tears ran down her cheeks.

The women ran outside and found Tommy laying on the ground. He was hollering and crying very loud and holding his arm. The snake had slithered away.

Jane scooped him up in her arms and carried him into Karry's bedroom and laid him on the bed, where he could be kept quiet. He became very feverish. A neighbor had gone into town to get John and the doctor. Meantime, Jane had put a fairly tight tourniquet three inches above the wound, on Tommy's arm to keep the poison from going into his blood system too fast. She also raised his arm onto a pillow, keeping it above his body.

The doctor couldn't do anything. Everything had been done that could be done. John and Jane took turns wiping Tommy's face with a cool cloth. Nothing helped. He slipped away during the night.

It took a long time after Tommy's funeral, before Jane and John had the will to carry on. They missed their little boy so much. She just stayed around home. The Martin's had been to visit and John and Jane assured them that it wasn't their fault. Tommy was a very inquisitive little boy and was very fast. There wasn't any blame to be put anywhere. This had just happened!

CHRISTMAS

Time went on and Tommy's death seemed to heal with it. Jane found herself expecting again. They were both excited and this seemed to give life a new meaning. They could hardly wait for the birth of their new baby.

On February 29th, 1876, leap year, Kathleen Ellen was born. She was a rolly polly little bundle and was soon spoiled by everyone.

John and Jane's family was started. Joseph Henry was born on December 17, 1877 just before Christmas. John thought that he looked like Tommy but he didn't say so. He just kept this thought to himself. He loved them all and didn't want to bring up any unhappy memories.

John always liked trains and was curious to how they worked. He was offered a railroad job in St. Mary's, Kansas, just a few miles north of Topeka. He would be working at a railroad switching station. When trains were coming through, he would switch the tracks so they went on different tracks to different destinations. He would also collect the mail.

This was a dirty outside job. It was cold and wet work. The train was something that was fairly new and it was far from perfect. It was seldom on time so he had to wait around until it arrived. Sometimes he would be waiting for hours.

It was at St. Mary's that their fourth child was born. Margaret Marie came into the world on March 12, 1880. She was a healthy girl with very good lungs.

He wished that he had given this more thought before he took the job. He had promised that he would stay at least a year. The money was very good and the house they lived in was free.

He would bring his feelings up to Jane and see what she thought of moving to Topeka when his year was finished. They had discussed getting back to the city life. They missed the people and working their clothing business.

"This job isn't anythin' that I thought it would be. I'm gone all hours and have to leave you and the kids alone too much. I have been doin' some thinkin' 'bout everthin'. How would you like to move into Topeka? We could look for a nice big house for us to live in."

"I could find a store on main street and start our clothin' business up again. You could work on doin' the ladies hats."

It didn't take much convincing on Jane's part. "I've hoped for along time that you'd want to move. This job is not for you. The kids and I miss you. When you aren't workin' then you're sleepin'. This isn't a good family life."

She was more than ready to move. "I've wanted to move to Topeka for some time now. It is a nice sized town to live in. The people are friendly."

A few days later, they packed up the children in the buggy and headed to town. They were looking for a nice house to live in. The day was happy. Everyone was in a festive mood with smiles on their faces. This hadn't happened for a while.

Before night fall, they had found a perfect house for themselves and the kids. A two story four bedroom house only a few blocks from main street. After locating the owner and making arrangements to buy the house, they went on to locate a shop area close by. They were getting very tired and decided to leave this until they were all moved.

John gave his notice to the railroad and Jane and the kids got busy packing everything up and getting it ready to move. Everyone was excited about moving back to the city life.

The kids kept asking questions. Were there other little kids there? What did city mean? Just to name a few.

One morning, John heard a lot of noise. As he opened the door he exclaimed "What is this?" Several rigs had been lined up and were ready to move the Taylor's to town. The men and their teenage boys were standing around just waiting to be told to start loading.

"Thought you would need some help movin' so here we are." said a burly man with a big grin.

The men loaded things out of the house and into the wagons. When they were loaded, they moved caravan style in to Topeka. As soon as everything was unloaded into the new house, the ladies promptly put things away. When this was done, the women brought out food and drinks. It was time for a party.

What wonderful people! They would never be forgotten!

Shortly after their move to Topeka, Jane discovered that she was again expecting. Child number five, Bessie Jean, was born March 2, 1882. They had a wonderful family. Life settled down. The clothing business was keeping John and Jane very busy. Jane made a hat once in awhile but John worked continuously.

Time just seemed to float by. The children were growing by leaps and bounds. Kathleen had started school and thought she was very important. Joe would start school next year.

In the next five years two more daughters were born. Nancy Anne joined her brothers and sisters on

May 27, 1885 and Jenny Isabel joined them on April 21, 1887.

Christmas was coming. The White's and the Taylor's were venturing down from Sioux City for the holidays and John, Jane and the children were very excited. Johnny and Catherine, along with their seven year old son, Joshua and their five year old daughter, Roberta would be coming too.

John and Jane had only seen the family a few times since moving to Kansas. They had taken a fast trip home when Maggie had gotten married and moved to Montana. Since then, Frank, Al, Gladys and Kate had all married. They weren't able to go to any of their weddings. Some day they planned an extended trip to go home and see everyone.

"How is everybody gonna' get here?" Joe asked his father.

"They will be takin' a Paddle boat from Sioux City to Kansas City, then the stage coach from Kansas City to Topeka. It will be a long, cold trip for them, I'm afraid."

Jane had hired a lady to come in and help with the cleaning and cooking. All the rugs were taken up, put on the clothes line and beat with a large paddle. Then they were aired and put back down. All the feather ticks and quilts were also aired. The house was cleaned from top to bottom.

John and the kids had gone out and cut down a large cedar tree to be used for their Christmas tree. There weren't very many around but John had found a few on a ridge behind their house. They decorated it with popcorn, cranberries, rings made from colored paper, and small candles. Jane had made a rag doll angel for the top. It now stood in the corner of the living room. Later it would be put in the center of the room, waiting for the pretty gifts and packages that would soon surround it.

Large stockings would be hung close to the tree after the children went to sleep.

Although Christmas wasn't celebrated by everyone to a great extent, the activity and hustle and bustle by the Taylor family put everyone into the Christmas and holiday spirit.

It was the morning of Christmas Eve and John was getting the horse and buggy ready to go meet the stagecoach.

"Can we go with you?" Kathleen and Joe asked their father. "Please, papa! Can we?"

"We wanna' go too!" Margaret and Bessie spoke up. "Can we?"

"I don't think there will be room for everyone coming back in the buggy if you come too." John explained."

Seeing the disappointment on their faces, he continued, "We won't be very long. We will go for a long ride while everyone is here. We will show them around the town and you two can be the guides. How about that?"

Although it wasn't what they wanted, they accepted the idea. Soon they were inside the house telling their mother, "Guess what? Papa said that we can go for a ride, maybe tomorrow. We get to show everyone around the town."

They were waiting impatiently for everyone to return from the stage coach.

"You will make good guides. But everyone will have to bundle up. It is really cold out there."

Suddenly the door opened. "Merry Christmas!" said Johnny as he followed Catherine and his mother into the house. Everyone followed them into the living room.

Everybody hugged and kissed. They were so glad to see each other again.

"We should unload the buggy before it gets any later." John took command and the guys unloaded the buggy. There was a lot of baggage for so many people. There were several different sizes of boxes among them.

Joe took charge of his new cousin Joshua immediately and the girls took charge of Roberta. Soon the children went outside and the adults settled in. Lunch was on the table and Christmas Eve was here. Last minute gifts were being put under the tree and everyone sang Christmas carols while Jane played the piano.

The children were getting sleepy. Jane said "Okay! Bedtime!"

She sent the older ones to bed and soon had the little ones saying their prayers and settled in for the night. When it was decided that the kids were asleep, the big presents were brought out and then everyone went to bed. It had been a long day and would certainly prove be a longer tomorrow.

Jane had sent to Chicago for the latest thing in dolls. She got each of the girls a doll with a porcelain face, hands and feet and she had made clothes for them. John had made them each a doll bed and a small vanity.

He had made each of the boys a sled. All the kids got kites, balls and other toys. John had made each child a new coat and Jane had made them each a new hat to go with it.

Christmas day had gone quickly. The children decided to sing Christmas carols around the neighborhood and the women thought it would be nice if they went along and sang with them. It was great fun. When they returned home, they had hot cocoa and cookies.

The days went by rapidly and soon it was time for the company to leave for Iowa and home.

"We hate to see everybody leave. It has been such a great time and we will miss everybody." Jane said. With promises of seeing everyone again and amidst the kisses and tears, they boarded the stage coach.

THOUGHTS OF THE WEST

John was coming home after a busy day at his shop. He worked hard to provide for his family and was able to put aside a sizable nest egg and was proud of all he had accomplished.

He was standing at the gate looking into his front yard at his two story home. It was a well built four bedroom white wood frame house surrounded by a white picket fence. Jane had made it into a nice place to live.

His mind began to wonder back over the events of the past week. He had been busy measuring material from a large bolt of colored cotton, when Jack Anderson entered the shop. John stopped what he was doing and asked "What can I do to help you, Jack?"

"I need you to make me a heavy duty wool suit that will last me a long time. I'm starting up a wagon train north of here and heading for Oregon."

John had had a secret dream to go west ever since the war. Maybe this was the way for this to happen. He had been mulling this over for a couple of days. When Jack came back for more measurements, John was waiting to find out more about the wagon trip.

While John took measurements, Jack explained. "I sold my house and blacksmith shop. I had enough money to buy wagons, oxen to pull 'em and a few cattle. Still gotta' buy seed to take along to plant. I hope to get some good bottom land. I have provisions to last a year for me, my wife and three boys."

"How do your wife and boys feel about this?" John inquired.

"My wife is adventurous but she had some misgivin's. Now the boys, they are ready anytime. Typical boys!"

"What's the land like? Is there lots of room? What's the weather like?"

"Well, I understand there are rich fertile lands from the ocean inland to the mountains. Plenty of room for ever'body. "I heard tell that the wild pigs are fully cooked with forks and knives in 'em so... when a person got hungry, he just started eatin'." At this point, Jack slapped his leg and laughed.

"When are you leavin' and when do you expect to get there?"

"We'll be leavin' around April first and hope to get there no later than the middle or end of September. We don't want to travel any later because of mountain terrain, snows, bad weather or any kind of hardships. Even September is pushing it."

John was not a frivolous person. He had to give this a lot of thought. He would have to sell everything he owned in Topeka, buy supplies and be ready to leave in four months.

He decided to check out a few things and then make his decision.

Entering a large shed, John was forced to step back. Both large doors were pushed open and a new Conestoga wagon was being pushed out of the shed where it would be harnessed up with four oxen. Once it was loaded, depending on the weight of the load, it could take as many as 24 oxen to pull it.

"Fancy piece of work!" John commented. "Jack Anderson sent me to talk to a fellow by the name of Charles Bateman. Jack claims that he is the best builder in these parts."

"That's me What can I do for you?" Charles asked. "Come on into my office and have some coffee. What do you need to know?"

Reaching into a drawer, he pulled out a picture of a prairie schooner and tossed it across the desk for John to look at.

"These are being used more now a days. It is half the size of a Conestoga wagon but you won't need so many live stock to pull it and they are a lot easier to work. Teams of 4-6 oxen or 6-10 mules are enough to pull a schooner all the way to Oregon. They are specially made so they can be raised two feet to travel over high water and larger rocks. They are 5' wide, 12' long, and 10' tall with the tight canvas bonnet held by hardwood bows but it's very sturdy. If it breaks down, it can easily be dismantled and repaired. They offer as good a shelter as a wood house."

"It might pay a man to take an extra schooner and not bother with the big wagon."

"Figure out three of the schooners. I'll be needin' two for freight and one for livin' purposes."

"I'll come by your shop tomorrow with the information and costs." Charles offered. "Then you can decide what you want to order."

"This sounds good to me." John said as he stood up to leave and shook Charles's hand. "I'll see you tomorrow then."

Having made up his mind, he decided that now was the time to discuss this with Jane. He hoped that she would like the idea and agree with him.

John walked through the front door like a man in a dream. Hanging his long coat and bowler hat, he called out. "Jane! Where are you?"

"I'm in the kitchen fixin' supper!" she yelled back at him. Six year old Bessie and three year old Nancy were on the floor playing with the baby Isabel. Joe was bringing firewood in from the back yard and filling the wood box behind the big black cook stove. Kathleen and Margaret were helping their mother.

John went into the kitchen. A warm comfortable place. The smell of fresh bread was teasing his appetite. Suddenly he remembered that he hadn't eaten since breakfast. With his mind full of dreams, he just hadn't been hungry but now he was famished and ready to eat.

The large oak table had been brought from Sioux City and was a gift from John's parents. It had eight large chairs, a sideboard and large cupboard to go with it. It now looked nice in the large dining room nestled off the kitchen.

Giving Jane a big hug and hugging the kids, except for Joe who thought he was too big for hugs, John called everyone to eat. After everyone was settled down, John said grace. The kids started talking all at once. The room seemed to come alive. "Jane, please quiet everybody down. I have something very important to talk to you all about. Joe, please don't tease Nancy! Everyone please be quiet."

"What would you think about moving west to Washington Territory? We would have to go by wagon train. I checked out the railroad trains. In order to have some money to work with when we get there, the fares would be too expensive for our budget." He went on to explain all that he had learned and answered all their many questions as well as he could.

Suddenly everyone was silent. Jane was stunned. She knew that John had been extra quiet for the last few days but had no idea what he was thinking. "What would you do when we got there? What are your plans?"

"I plan to buy some land, and raise my own cattle. I'll take seed and probably grow most of my own feed and vegetables. I'll always have my trade to fall back on and we'll take all our machines with us and also take a good supply of materials, too."

"It sounds like a wonderful thing to do. We really have to discuss this, John, but let me think about it for a couple of days. Then we will discuss it further." Jane said. "This has taken me completely by surprise."

John knew that if he just waited that Jane would be ready to go along with him.

HEADIN' OUT

April first started off as a very cold and busy morning. The men had been working since early the night before lining up the forty five schooners and the freight wagons and making everything ready for their start to Oregon.

Jack Anderson was riding his big gray horse from wagon to wagon making sure all was loaded properly and not overloaded. Because of this, lots of things such as heavy furniture was given away or left there for someone to pick up and take home. He explained that it was better done now rather than later on the trail. It would get to be too heavy a load for the animals to pull.

The kids, sleepy and cranky, were being tucked all into the same bed in each of the schooners. The men were yelling back and forth to each other, dogs were barking and the live stock was bawling and making a fuss and the horses were neighing. It was a noisy undertaking. It would quiet down as soon as they started and everything became routine.

All the last names were put into a hat and as each name was drawn out, that person fell into line behind Jack. This put John's schooner in third place. This would prove to be hot and dirty as the trip progressed. The heat and dirt would be disturbed and fly into the following schooners. These people would soon be covered with dirt. Because of this, each wagon would stay at least four wagon lengths behind the one ahead of it.

Each party had a saddle horse. This was decided to be an important thing when it came to looking for food later on the trail. All the freight wagons were brought up at the end of the train so that the people themselves were kept fairly close together.

At the first sight of daylight, Virginia, Jack's wife, driving their wagon started the team forward and each wagon started accordingly. Jack rode along checking each wagon as it pulled out making sure that all was well.

"This is a wonderful feelin', John, and at the same time it is very scary. The kids are happy about it all but Joe was askin' if they would be going to school there. I told him that if there wasn't a school around, that I would teach them. I really think that he thought there wouldn't be any more school." Jane remarked as she rode beside her husband on the seat of their new schooner. "There can't be any lookin' back now!"

John agreed with her. "Lookin' back over the months, I can hardly believe all that we accomplished. Bein' able to sell our house and property as we did made it easier."

"Everything went smoothly. Sellin' the shop and trainin' the people to operate it was a good thing too. It was a nice challenge. Now we can go ahead with our plans and not have to worry about anything here. It has all been done. Of course we will miss our friends but maybe we'll see them again someday."

"Now we can just concentrate on where we are going and what we will be doing from this point on."

Traveling northwest from Topeka, Kansas to Fort Kearney, Nebraska was flat, dry, and sandy prairie lands.

Riding along at a fair pace and everything going as well as could be, John and the family were getting used to the slow pace and staying far enough behind the wagon in front of them. There was very little communication with other people unless they stopped. The children, women, and dogs walked and played beside the moving wagons during the day.

Jack came riding back and asked John to get his horse and go with him. Stopping the oxen, John handed the reins to Jane, and jumped to the ground. Going around the back he untied his horse, climbed on and followed Jack.

"I've been watching the sky. There is a large black cloud right in our path. I've heard stories about the terrible wind storms. Seems we can try to go around it, but this will take us miles and days out of our way. We can stay here and wait it out or continue on and see if it goes another direction. I need your thoughts on this."

"We can't try to go around. This would put us at risk farther on for our arrival time and the mountains." John said. "Maybe we should continue on and hope the winds change course. We can warn the families and have them hamper everything down in case we get caught. We would be settin' ducks if we just waited it out."

"This is about what I figured.." Jack said. "I'm goin' to ask the Larson family to change places with your wagon in the line. I've been watchin' you, John. You have a good head on your shoulders. I'll be needin' you behind me if we run into any problems."

John agreed and they turned their horses and rode back to the wagons. Jack rode forward and talked to Lars and then went on, halting the wagons. John tied up his horse, climbed into the rig and took the reins from Jane.

He explained to her what was happening and went on to discuss his change in roles. "Could you handle the rig? Jack has asked me to kinda be his second in command, just in case I'm needed. I would drive the wagon most of the time and anytime the goin' gets bad. Others will be close by too. We will be helpin' each other."

"I think I can handle the team. They're pretty well used to the road now." She answered. "You'll always be close in case."

Then he pulled his rig out of line and moved it forward to take Larson's place. Larson pulled his rig out of the line and waited until the other rigs were brought forward and left an empty spot for his rig. Several of the men were helping with this shifting of the wagons. It wasn't easy to do and the children all had to be kept in the wagons out of the way.

When this was accomplished it was getting towards dark. Jack decided they should circle the wagons and settle in for the night.

Everyone was fed and the wagons reloaded. The children were put to bed. The men were setting around the cook fire discussing the days maneuvers. All of a sudden the wind began howling and the wagons started to rock. The men, women and children got under the wagons for safety. The animals had been tied down earlier and were snorting and bawling and trying to get loose. This lasted for only a few minutes.

Jack and John along with other men, began to investigate the damages. Canvases had been pulled from several wagons and were hanging down the side. One of the wagons had been overturned and the contents were strewn everywhere. No one had been hurt. The livestock eventually calmed down.

The wagon was immediately up righted and beds were made in the other wagons for the family. The next morning when there was daylight to see by, repairs were started. Beginning with the over turned wagon, all the things that hadn't been blown away were found and again packed away in the wagon. Canvasses were again pulled tight on the schooners. All possible repairs were made. When all was done they spent the rest of the day relaxing. The next morning they again were on their way.

Stopping at Hastings, Nebraska, they pulled in and camped on the edge of town, next to the Little Blue

River. They spent the next day replenishing the water supply and getting any supplies that they needed. They checked the rigs and make any repairs and the women spent the day washing clothes and airing the bedding.

The next morning they were on their way to Fort Kearney, Nebraska. They would be spending several days there to get major supplies and food stuffs and extra things they may need. It would be weeks before they came to Fort Laramie and they didn't want to get caught short.

They brought food stuffs from Topeka with them. They figured a hundred and fifty pounds of flour per person. Flour was hard to come by on the trail. If they did find any, it was of very poor quality. They brought five pounds of baking powder for biscuits, soda, corn meal, hardtack and crackers were used as a variety. Forty pounds of sugar per person was stored in rubber sacks to prevent it getting wet. Forty-five pounds of smoked bacon packed in strong sacks and covered with bran, and ten pounds of jerky per person. Rice and beans were cooked when they had lots of fuel. Thirty or forty pounds of dried fruit and vegetables per person were strung from the bows of the wagons. Other items were molasses, potatoes, tea, coffee and whiskey. The coffee was used the most because it covered the bad taste of the waters. All meals were easy to fix. Cattle, not to be used to start a herd later, were brought along for eating. The men and older boys planned hunting parties for deer and wild game. They wouldn't wander very far. The boys loved to go fishing and usually brought a large catch for a meal.

Water was carried in large forty-gallon casks that were lashed to the side of a wagon and kept filled when they could. It was the most important thing that they worried about.

At seven o'clock all teamsters were ready to move out. A few notes from a bugle were sounded and the lead wagon moved out and like clock work the others follow, one by one.

The children collected little treasures as they walked along, such as pretty rocks, turtles, and flowers. They played Indian and soldier and had snowball fights with buffalo chips. Each child walked no less than fifteen miles a day.

The wagon train stopped about eleven o'clock for a break. This was called nooning. It was the hottest time of the day and they would use it to eat and rest for awhile. Then they would travel on until dark.

MOUNTAINS & INDIANS

One night just as they were starting supper, Lars came up to the wagon. "Jane, I wonder if you would come to our wagon. Our little Deloris is very sick and Erma sent me to ask if you would come."

Putting down the pot she was holding, she told the girls what to warm up for supper. "I need to go check on Deloris and help Erma. If I am away too long, you all go ahead and eat. Dad, is helpin' Jack, so go get him when it's ready and let him know what I am doin'."

Jane and Lars walked back to his wagon. He opened the flap and helped Jane get inside where Erma and the sick little girl were.

"Thank you for comin'." Erma said as she wrung out a cloth that she was dipping in water and putting on her little girls face. "She wasn't feelin' very well last night but we thought maybe it wasn't anything special. You know how kids are? But durin' the night, she got very feverish and clammy and vomited quite a lot. She has been in bed all day. Her fever seemed to break but now she is getting' hot again. I don't have any idea what it could be. Must have been something that she caught in Hastings."

"I found some real pretty red berries and I ate 'em and they were good, mama, but they made me sick." Deloris spoke up. "They made my tummy hurt real bad."

Jane, seeing the problem asked, "Do you have some soda? Get two glasses and fill one with water. Add a teaspoon of soda to the water. Pour the soda water back and forth until it is mixed real good."

After Erma had fixed the soda water, Jane said "Have Deloris drink as much as she can. This should help her settle her tummy ache and maybe she will start to feel better. Give her another dose in the morning.

I'll come back before we pull out and check on her but if you need me in the night, send Lars to get me. Hopefully this will do it."

"Thank you," Erma said "I was about at my wits end. I'll keep sponging' her. She doesn't seem so warm now either. We will have to let everybody know about this so the kids won't be pickin' and eatin' the berries. Could have some real sick kids."

As Jane walked towards their wagon, she could hear the men talking about the trip ahead. Entering the group, she explained, "Little Deloris Larson was a pretty sick little girl. Seems as though she found some pretty red berries and ate em'. We'll have to let everybody know." She moved on to the wagon. The children were in bed but they had left her some beans with salt back and bread. She fixed herself a plate, quickly ate and went on to bed.

Following the North Platte River from Fort Kearney to Fort Laramie, a distance of 330 miles, the travelers passed many land marks and stopped long enough to write their names on the rocks. One such landmark was Chimney Rock at Scott's Bluff, Nebraska. The train rested for a nooning. The men gathered and talked, while the children played.

They stayed for several days at Fort Laramie. During this time, they again replenished supplies, made all repairs, washed clothes, rested and visited. Everybody got a chance to learn all the news from all directions.

The next leg of their journey was going up into the mountains. The going would be hard and slow. The dangers were always there. Not only from unforeseen hardships but from wild animals and the Indians.

A warning had been sent out to all travelers. Renegade Indians were uprising along the trail and all should be well armed and prepared. It was hard to believe that they would attack a train this size but no one could be sure. The Indians had the advantage of knowing the terrain and water holes. They would also try to get to the livestock. This would mean extra men riding the rear and having around the clock sentries. It was better to be prepared than to be caught unawares.

Jack Anderson had heard at the store about a mountain man named Zeak. He was looking to hire onto a wagon train and work as a guide. Seemed that he had been about everywhere.

Jack came around the edge of the wagon and hollered at John. "Could you come into town this afternoon with me? I need to go to the saloon and look for a man named Zeak. He claims to be a great guide and I thought that I would have a talk with him and if all works out, have him come along with us."

John had been sharpening knives for Jane. A job that he had been promising to do for weeks and didn't seem to find time for. "Well, guess they will wait a little longer." He said to himself.

He sent Joe to tell Jane where he had gone.

"It seems that we might have a rough time and havin' an experienced guide along with us could spare us a lot of troubles later on. What do you think'?" Jack said to John.

"This might just be the answer to some of our prayers." John answered.

Getting his horse from the staked in area, he saddled him, and rode over and met Jack just as he was getting ready to leave.

Going inside, the saloon was dark until they had been there a few minutes so their eyes could adjust. A poker game was going on with four players at a table just off from the bar. A couple guys were leaning up against it.

Walking up to it, Jack ordered a beer for John and one for himself. Looking around, he seen a lone guy setting at a table across the room.

"See that guy over there? Is his name Zeak?" Jack asked the bartender. "I'm looking for a guide and was told he'd be here."

"That's him! Stays around here most of the time." he answered. "Quiet fellow. Stays to himself."

Taking their beer with them, and another for Zeak, they walked over to the table.

Putting the beer in front of the man, Jack asked, "Your name, Zeak?" The man nodded his head, yes. "I understand that you know the mountains from here to Oregon, like the back of your hand. Is this right?"

"I been all over the hills and mountains. Lived as a mountain man for thirty years." Zeak answered. "Pull out a chair and set down."

Jack introduced himself and John. "I'm taking a wagon train to Oregon. We've come from Topeka, Kansas. I heard that you are a great guide and Indian man. You was heard telling that you would like to guide a wagon train and go to Oregon. Is this right?"

"I sure would, mister." he said. "What are you lookin' for and what're you offerin?"

After talking everything over, Zeak agreed to meet them first thing in the morning. A freight wagon would be repacked to make room for him to have a place to bed down and he'd take his meals with the Anderson's. He had been hired on and was ready to go.

They left Fort Laramie and the safety of the big fort very early in the morning. Following the South Platte River, they moved on to Independence Rock and the Sweetwater River. The going got rougher. Because of the rocky terrain, the river had to be crossed. This was not easy. The oxen had to be led into the water and they balked and tried to run taking the wagon with them. After the first wagon got across, the rest seemed to take it easier as they followed.

The alkali in the water poisoned the cattle. Zeak suggested that they force bacon and grease down the throats of the animals. This saved most of the animals.

Suddenly the rivers were flowing westward and they realized that they had crossed the continental divide.

It was decided to take the short cut through the valley to Fort Bonneville. They would rest there for a few days before moving on.

"Look up ahead!" one of the lookouts yelled to John as he came by on his way to warn Jack.

Clouds of dust were being raised by horses. All at once, the warning came through, "Circle the wagons. Bring the beef and livestock inside the circle. Hurry! Indians! Indians."

The wagons were circled. Many of the women and older boys were good shots and used the rifles and helped the men. Other women and older children loaded the guns and some of the older children helped keep the smaller children down out of harms way. The livestock were bawling and trying to get out of the circle but most of them had been staked down.

Several of the Indians had been shot and one of the men close to Jane had been shot in the leg. Looking around she saw another man holding his arm. She looked around for John and seeing him a couple wagons away, unharmed, she went back to loading guns.

Suddenly the Indians rode off as fast as they had come. Everybody stayed where they were to be sure that they were gone for good.

Jane found the children and made sure they were safe and hadn't been hurt. She then got her medicine bag and along with other women went to work helping the wounded.

A scout was sent to Fort Bonneville to get an army escort to take them on into the fort. The men talked it over and decided that it was probably safer to stay where they were until the escort arrived.

They used this time to rest or repair canvases that had been torn with the Indian arrows. The livestock had been fed and settled down.

LOST BOYS

After arriving at Fort Bonneville late in the day, the Fort Commander, Captain Collins, told Jack and John about a terrible Indian massacre at Soda Springs, a spot they would have to travel through. An army troop would escort them part way through the area. A scout would be sent to Fort Hall and a troop would be sent out to meet them and take them on to the fort.

John told the family that the Captain suggested leaving at first daylight. He wanted to get started as soon as possible. Any supplies they needed, they would try to get at Fort Hall. There would be no time to get things here.

The next morning, moving out of the fort with the troop was quite an adventure. All the children had been told to stay in the wagons during the trip to Fort Hall. This made it hard for them but safety came first. The troop would stop often so they could get out, walk around and exercise their legs.

The kids mostly behaved themselves but they were tending to get cranky and fuss with each other as the trip continued on. Billy and Kathleen took charge of the younger kids, making sure that they were fed and taken care of. This left Jane free to drive the team and help in other ways.

During one of these break times, everyone was gathering around the campfire for their noon meal.

John asked "Where is Billy? Has anybody seen him?" Apparently he hadn't been seen since the wagon train had stopped.

Suddenly Virginia, appeared and walked up to John. Have you seen Wes? Nobody has seen him since we stopped."

"Billy is gone too. They must be together." John had a sick feeling that they were in the mountains.

"They can't be to far.", he went on.

A search party was gathered and soon some of the men and soldiers were going in different directions into the hills searching for the missing boys. By night fall, they hadn't been found. It was to dark to see anything.

Jane fed everyone and sent the kids to bed early. They quieted down with their own thoughts. They were as worried as their Mom and Dad. They had visions of their brother being eaten by wild animals or the Indians getting them.

The men paced back and forth and talked about what might have happened. They hoped that they hadn't been taken by renegade Indians. Not only this but the wild animals were also a great threat. The search would resume early in the morning. Jane was frantic! All she could do was wait and see.

Billy and Wes were standing below some big trees throwing rocks at the branches.

"I wonder what is up on that hill." Billy said. "Should we go and see?"

"Maybe we shouldn't. Might get lost. Let's don't." Wes said very nervously. "I'm scared of the bears and Indians."

"We'll just go to the top of the hill. We'll be able to see the wagons. Come on Fraidy Cat!" he said as he started up the hill into the trees.

Wes was right behind him. He was afraid to go and afraid to turn back.

They climbed up and around a hill and became lost. They could no longer see the wagons. Realizing that they were lost, they decided to try and find their way back through the trees. They wandered around for a long time. Wes started complaining that he was hungry and thirsty. Billy tried to reassure him that the army would come and look for them and bring food and water.

The sun went down early in the trees and it soon became very dark. The boys hung onto each other so they wouldn't become separated. They sat down at the base of a large pine tree and tried to rest. Billy couldn't sleep right away but soon Wes was cuddled up to him fast asleep. Here they stayed the night.

The next morning they woke up with someone shaking them. A grizzled old man with long hair and a large matted beard was looking down at the two of them.

"Wake up you two! Been here all night? Are you the ones that those army fellers are lookin' for? You must be cold and hungry." he guessed.

"We just went lookin' around." Billy told him. "All of a sudden we couldn't see the wagons. We tried to get back through the trees and then we really got mixed up!"

"Well, come on! I'll set you on the right track so you can get back okay. I 'magine your folks are plenty worried by now." He turned and walked into the trees and the boys were right behind him.

The boys soon realized just how far they had wondered around lost. It must have been several miles. The old man stopped and pointed to a trail going down the hill. It wasn't much of a trail. One that was used by wild animals.

"Stay on this and don't turn around. You will be okay. It goes down and around this hill and will bring you out to where you'll see the wagons in the distance."

The boys did as the old man told them. Billy suddenly remembered to thank him, but the old man was gone. He just seemed to disappear as though he was never there.

Coming out of the trees, they spied the wagons about a quarter of a mile ahead. Running as fast as they could, falling down, getting up and in general falling over their own feet in their rush to get into camp.

Billy grabbed Jane and hugged her. Everyone was trying to talk at once. They were telling everyone about getting lost and how sorry they were that they had worried everybody. They promised never to do this again.

Turning to his father, he told him about the grizzled old man. An army sergeant standing close by explained that this old man had been around for many years. He was a hermit and wanted to be left alone. Very few people saw him. It was very lucky for the boys that he decided to step in and help.

John took Billy aside. He told him how glad he was that they had been found and how worried everyone had been. He then gave him a very stern talking to and extra chores to do. This would keep him busy and he wouldn't have time to get into mischief.

The word was passed that the boys were back and safe. All search parties soon returned to the camp. After a short rest, the troop and the wagons soon started on again.

After several hours, a large cloud of dust gave warning of riders coming. The Captain put up his hand to bring a stop to everything. Soon it was apparent that the troop had arrived to take the wagon train on into Fort Hall.

Jack and Captain Collins were talking when John walked up to them. "Guess this is good bye", John said to the Captain. "It has been a great trip travelin' with you. We all thank you and your men for all you have done. Especially lookin' for our boys."

"You are welcome. You have fine families and boys will be boys when given the chance. Just real happy that they returned unhurt. Lots of Indians, wild animals and just plain trouble in the mountains. They were lucky to be found by the old man. So long." he said as he shook hands with each of the men. He mounted his horse and gave the signal to ride.

Jane and John stood watching for a long time as Captain Collins and his men turned around and rode back the way they had come.

Jack, with John by his side, walked over to where Captain Forest was waiting. Shaking hands all around they introduced themselves and thanked them for coming.

"Fort Hall is small but durable. There isn't much there." The Captain explained. "But it is safe."

"Will we be able to get supplies?" Some one asked.

The Captain answered. "We can give you some supplies to help until you get to Boise. Boise is a good sized settlement and you can get about anything you need."

He and his troop then moved in and took over as though nothing had happened. The wagons were soon moving as though nothing had changed.

They arrived at Fort Hall just before dark. After everyone had been fed and the children down for the night, the women sat around camp fires and discussed the events of the day. What was most on everyone's minds was the shortage of food and other supplies. They decided to ration what supplies they had. Anything they might have a lot of they would share with other families. This should see them through to Boise.

Because of the shortage of supplies, Jack had a meeting of the men and it was decided that they wouldn't stay. At sun-up, they would check all the wagons and livestock. They had been on a fairly fast pace with little time to do this. They wanted to be sure all was well.

This didn't take long and soon the wagons were rolling out the gates of Fort Hall on their way. The trip was uneventful. The settlers at Boise had made peace with the Indians long ago and were living in harmony.

The weather was nice but starting to get cooler. Nobody seemed concerned about it. They still had plenty of time before winter set in.

Entering the settlement was a surprise. It was spread out into the wilderness. It had become the capital of the Idaho territory.

Jack decided that this would be a good time to make camp and give the women a chance to shop and wash clothes and air things out. The men needed to make repairs.

Jane and Virginia along with Kathleen could hardly wait to go shopping. They seemed to need a lot of things. Jane bought pants for the older boys and a couple of dresses for Kathleen. They seemed to grow up fast since leaving Kansas. They wouldn't be children much longer. The rest of the children could wear hand-me-downs until they got where they were going. Lots of things could be mended until that time. It shouldn't be very long before the trip was over.

They found a large store and were able to get fresh fruit and vegetables. This was a real treat. They bought sugar and flour and other supplies.

Jane was excited. The smell of leather hung in the air. "I can't believe this place. It reminds me of my dad's place in Iowa." She suddenly got choked up. "It just seems to have a little bit of everything that a person could need."

She suddenly felt very unhappy thinking about her family. She thought about them often and wondered what they were doing and when she would see them again. Little things that happened made her think of them. She suddenly realized just how much she missed her family and friends. Every so often John and the kids would mention something that reminded them of an incident that had happened which seemed so long ago.

They settled in for several days. The women cooked and washed clothes. The beds were pulled apart and all the bedding thrown out over the wagons to air out.

Repairs were made to the wagons. The animals were given a chance to rest. The men were able to talk about things they had seen and where they had been.

An old man got out his fiddle and started to play. Soon a couple started dancing and before long several people were dancing and having fun. The kids joined in. One of the guys found a jug of whiskey and passed it around among the men. They felt good. Dancing was a past time among the pioneers on the wagon train. The music and getting together was their way to forget the hardships for a little while. They did a lot of it.

In two days they would be leaving and going on their way. The men were worried about crossing the Snake River. They had been told that it was a terrible ordeal and people had lost everything they owned trying to cross. Jack and John had many discussions with the townspeople on how to cross.

They spent hours making decisions that would affect every wagon in the train. The safety of every man, woman and child, and getting all the live stock across without losing one. This was going to be the hardest part of the trip so far.

CROSSIN' THE SNAKE

"**P**ull the teams up tight! Keep 'em moving! Make sure they are in a straight line!" The orders were being yelled out. They had reached the Snake River last night and had camped just above it.

Jack and John rode out to explore and see what had to be done to get across the river. Their hearts sank as they soon realized that the only way to the river was down a very steep hill for about five hundred feet.

They called a meeting. Everybody was apprehensive. After explaining what they had found, it was decided to 'rough lock' the wheels on the wagons so they wouldn't turn, then skid them down the hill to the river below. Then they would put the families on them and float them across the river. They would take two days to do this half the train now and the other half the next day.

Everyone knew that it would be hard work and dangerous. They also knew that they had no choice. They had come too far and there wasn't any turning back.

A wagon was being skidded down the hill when the wheels began to turn and it veered away from the men that were holding it. A man tried to jump out of it's way but got tangled up in the ropes. He was run over and killed instantly. He left behind his wife and two small children.

The teams were herded down the hill where they were fastened together, putting the weakest in the middle. Jack carried one end of the rope and swam his horse to the other side. Guided by the rope, others on horseback followed until enough men were across, enabling them to pull the teams across.

The river was full of undercurrents. It was easy for a man or beast to be pulled under, never to be seen again. The Snake River was known as one of the most treacherous rivers ever heard of.

Some of the stock stampeded to the water edge to get a drink. A few swam across the river, and some had been swept under. It became a big task to keep them away from the water and keep them from stampeding to get to it. It was dangerous work and it took many men to keep them circled.

It took several days to get everything across the river. There was also lots of damage to the wagons. Several days were spent making repairs and putting everything right. They were all thankful that everything had gone as well as it had.

Several people had been banged up and bruised. One man had broken his arm while trying to turn a yoke of oxen.

The man had been buried. Jack had asked a single man that he knew if he would take over helping the young widow with her team and wagon while they were in route. She would feed him and he would look after her and her family.

The next morning early, the train was again on it's way. It followed the Snake River for many miles, until the river seemed to disappear into the rocks of the huge

Blue Mountains where a person couldn't follow. They rested in the foot hills a day and then started the long hard treacherous climb through the mountains. They could feel the coolness of the higher altitude as they climbed.

Moving along at a slow pace, a couple of the older boys decided to explore. Remembering the boys that got lost, they kept the wagons in sight. They were enjoying their walk when suddenly they heard a growl and a large brown bear appeared in their path. They screamed and ran toward the wagons with the bear right behind them.

Suddenly they heard shots and turning they saw the bear fall to the ground. Much further and the bear would have caught one of the boys. The wagon train had stopped and several of the men came running.

The boys were shook up but other wise they weren't hurt.

The man who shot the bear, decided to skin it, keeping the skin for himself. It was a valuable thing to have and later would be made into a rug. It would always be a subject to talk about later.

The bear was then butchered and the meat was distributed among several families that were less fortunate than others. At this time into the trip, supplies were certainly running low and so was the money and means. The meat was very welcome and appreciated.

Coming out of the mountains was a great feeling and being on flatter land made the travel easier and therefore the pace was faster. There would be no more mountains. Everyone was getting excited. They knew that they were getting close to the end of their journey. They followed the Umatilla River for a while and then turned straight west towards 'The Dalles' and the Columbia River.

They had just stopped for the night when they were approached by two men traveling alone. The men were heading towards Tacoma, Washington Territory. John invited them to eat dinner.

While eating, they talked about having jobs waiting for them. Large timber outfits were moving in and looking for experienced help, and the pay was better than anywhere else. Railroads were being built through the area and they were looking to hire men on.

There was lots of fishing. Hundred-pound salmon were being caught right there in the waters along with lots of other fish and sea foods. The climate was great. Seldom was there any cold weather.

The more they talked, the more John listened. John asked them to spend the night and travel along with them until the men headed north.

"What do you think, Jane?" he asked after they had gone to bed. "I have experience in both railroadin' and timber. We would have somethin' to at least look forward to. Goin' all the way to the coast would be nice to, I guess. But I would have to look for work and we aren't sure what we'd find. Of course we always have the shop we can set up."

"I think it makes more sense to go where you know they are lookin' for help. Sounds good to me." Jane answered. "When will you be tellin' Jack? I'm sure he'll understand. The goin' will be fairly good now that there won't be any more mountains. He won't need so much help."

"Will you be takin' over the train?" she continued. "I couldn't help hearin' what is bein' said. It's bein' said that the people want you to take 'em to Tacoma."

"I probably will. Somebody has to be in charge. I guess I have more experience than any of 'em. It won't be easy on you. It'll leave you and the kids pretty much on your own." John answered.

"We'll manage." Jane said as she feel asleep.

There had been talk and mutterings among the travelers ever since the men had showed up. Several people were ready to pull their wagons, leave the wagon train and go along with them.

Later on Jack asked nonchalantly, "Well, John! What do you think? Do you think we will lose many wagons?"

"Well since you brought it up. Jane and I have been seriously considerin' crossin' the Columbia below 'The Dalles'. There are several men that have approached me askin' my advice. Of course every one of 'em has to make their own decision on this and not everybody has the experiences to find work like I have. I do know that at least fifteen families are ready to cross the

173

Columbia River." he explained to Jack, what he and Jane had discussed.

"This is a surprise! Would you take over as wagon-master and take the train on to Tacoma? You'd make a good wagon-master and the people look up to you. They will follow you without any trouble. They will be needin' your help and leadership."

"We have learned well on this trip, haven't we Jack? It has been great traveling with you and your Mrs. and the kids. Our families have gotten very close. We won't be that far apart I guess and we can keep in touch." answered John.

Jack slapped John on the back and wished him well. They continued reminiscin' for awhile. Then they walked away to their own wagon to tell their families the news. At this time John had firmly made up his mind to go north to Tacoma rather than to the coast of Oregon.

SPLITTIN' UP THE TRAIN

As the Columbia River, at the Dalles, roared on, it became fast rapids and high winds. The steep rock walls made the area impassible and treacherous. It wasn't possible to move the train through this area. Earlier Jack had sent two of the guys to look for a place to cross. It was decided that they would move the train just above the Dalles close to the mouth of the Deschutes River.

Lewis and Clark had crossed here and several other wagon trains had floated their wagons across at this point. It was decided that this was the place to cross.

Jack brought the wagons to a halt. This was a good spot to get everything organized for the split of the train. Climbing down from his horse, he walked over to where John was getting down from his horse.

"Well, John, I guess this is a good place to start pullin' the wagons out and formin' new lines. You know I wish you all the luck in the world."

"This is gonna be a whole new life and none of us knows what's in the future. You ever get up our way or decide to come visit, we'll always have room for you and yours." John answered.

"You too!" Jack said as they shook hands and gave each other a hug. They then walked away giving orders to the guys to start moving the wagons.

A bearded man was operating a ferry. It was pulled across the river with large ropes and pulleys. He used long poles to keep the ferry lined up. John made a deal with him to take wagons and livestock across. One wagon with oxen was all that could cross at one time.

John had a meeting with his people. Everybody would help each other move the wagons and the livestock. Lars was asked to pull in behind John's wagon. The day was spent pulling wagons out of the train and forming a train to go north. As before, a day was spent making everything ready to cross. The excitement was building.

Someone brought out the fiddle and started playing. Someone else started playing the banjo and soon there was music and dancing. It was time to celebrate for what was probably the last time on the trail.

At day break, the wagons were being loaded onto the ferry and several large rafts were brought in to help carry the livestock.

"Lars, will you help Jane move our wagon forward onto the ferry. Then pull yours in line next. Keep the wagons moving forward." John said. "Be sure and watch the brakes on 'em. Shove big boulders inside the wheel so they can't move around."

Only a few at a time were able to cross. Once across, they started following the river on the Washington side. After all wagons were across, John stopped the train. It was beautiful, to look back and see where they had been.

They spent the rest of the day and the next day, making repairs and resting. While talking to different people during the loading, John learned that a good route would be to follow the Columbia River to Fort Vancouver.

As the train moved across the hills, getting closer to Fort Vancouver, the people were able to see the town and the ocean. The lands were tamed and the people were modern. The town was much larger than they expected. A small city had grown up. They were able to see their first wood frame house since leaving Kansas. As they moved into town, they passed many large stores.

The Columbia River flowed into the Pacific Ocean. They could see the water reaching into the horizon. They had never seen so much water before. It was kind of scary and took their breath away.

Jane and John sat on the sand watching the large birds. The water seemed to be everywhere. They hadn't had much chance to be together or to see anything.

"I hadn't thought that I would ever see anythin' as wide as the Missouri River. It is hard to imagine." Jane said.

"I never dreamed that there was so much water and that it would be so peaceful." he said. "There is a large fishing boat over there. This must be a great life."

"I wonder what is on the other side of the ocean!" Jane spoke up.

The next morning, Jane decided to go shopping and get what ever they needed to finish their trip into Tacoma. They wouldn't need as much as they had in the past but they had run short on necessary things.

"Kathleen, do you want to go with me to get supplies? I thought I would go this morning and check out the stores and the town and ask Erma to come along."

Kathleen had been pulling the bedding from the wagon so it could be airing out. "Yes, I want to go," she answered excitedly. "I'll be with you in a minute, mom."

While Jane stood waiting for Kathleen, she realized that their journey was about over. She could hardly wait to live in a real house again. The kids had been asking her if they were getting close yet? Now she would be able to tell them.

What would Tacoma be like? She had heard that it was a very large city. She was sure that John wouldn't have any trouble finding work.

The excitement spread through the camp. Hopefully the train would be in Tacoma with in a week.

John and Lars walked through the camp, checking on the repairs being done. Most of the wagons were looking rough and in bad shape. They had been repaired so many times and had endured many treacherous storms and miles. John couldn't believe that some of the wagons were so bad that they were still being repaired and still able to be used. Hopefully they would last another hundred miles or until they got to Tacoma.

"Could you use some help?" John asked one man that was attempting to fix a wheel. "Here let me hold this for ya!"

He helped another guy repair some harness that had worn thin and needed to be reinforced.

The two days went by fast, with everyone busy repairing things and the women were busy cooking. Soon it was time to start on the last leg of their journey.

The wagons were traveling on at a good pace. As bedraggled and beat up as they were, they were still usable. Some of them started out brand new but were now a very used commodity. They would soon be a large part of history. If they could talk, the story would be priceless.

The people were very excited! They were wanting to get to Tacoma. Once there, they still faced the tasks of making homes for their families, and finding jobs. Others were wanting to buy land and plant crops. This was to be home to all of them. This is what they had endured the hardships for.

TACOMA

The wagons were moving along at a good pace. Coming over the top of a hill and surrounded by water, the people were more than excited. It was September 15, 1888. They had made the long hard and some times cruel trek across the country. They had accomplished this before the winter had set in. The town spread before them for miles. It had become a railroad center for the Northern Pacific Railroad. Large lumber barons had sawmills and large lumber holdings. Coal mining was going on. Large shipping companies started up on the water front. Tacoma became known as the "City of Destiny". Some one had said that the population was around 35,000. Jobs and employment were plentiful. Truly it was the land of opportunity.

The wagons spread across the horizon as they started down the last mile into their new future. They had truly reached their destiny. John sent Lars ahead to look for a spot where they could camp once they got into town. They would be working out of the camp. Each family making their own way, looking for housing and employment.

John put his hand up to stop the wagons. He wanted them to look around so they would remember what it was like when they first arrived. It was a beautiful, wonderful sight. They could see wood frame houses and white fences, among the different types of tall evergreen trees. The large cedar trees seemed to stand out with their lacey dark green branches. Just beyond this was the great waters of the Puget Sound.

John moved his horse close to his wagon so he could talk to Jane. "What do you think?" he asked her. "Ain't this somethin'?"

"I can hardly believe we are here. I think I am in shock. This is the most wonderful feelin'." Jane replied.

The kids were out of the wagon and walking around. They were all talking at once. The excitement was in the air. Bill and Kathleen were asking a thousand questions. "Let's get goin'!," he said. "I just want to get there! Can we, dad?"

John put up his hand again to let the people know that they were moving on. One by one the wagons were soon moving down the hill into Tacoma.

"I'm gonna locate the two young fellows that headed us in this direction in the first place. I can't remember their names. Can you?" John hadn't had much time for socializing. "I want to catch 'em before they take off. Thought maybe I'd go along with 'em and meet this lumberman that had hired 'em. Wanna be first to see about a job." John was talking to Jane.

"Bob and Pat." she answered as she gave John a big hug. "The blond serious guy is Bob. Pat is the funny red head. Go now and I'll have something cooked when you get back."

John left, looking for Bob and Pat. Finding them getting their gear together, he walked up. "When are you headin' out to see your guy at the lumber company?

Do you mind if I tag along? I need work right away. Maybe the guy is hirin'. At least it is a place to start."

"Come along with us." Bob said. "We will be leavin' in a little bit. Just wanna say goodbye to a few friends we've made. We especially want to thank you and your wife. You've all made our trip so much easier. Anythin' we can do, just let us know."

Soon John, Bob, Pat and several other men were riding towards a large lumber mill and yard on the edge of town. They were all hoping to find work.

Bob asked a man to point out a Mr. Flynn. While everyone waited, Bob went to see him and let him know they were there. He would also talk to him about John and the rest of the guys. Soon Bob returned with a short muscular man. "This is Mr. Flynn, the foreman. The guys call him Flynn."

Turning to the foreman, he introduced each of the men from the wagon train. He told him about John and how well liked he was and how he had led the wagon train into Tacoma.

"What kinda work have you done?" he asked.

John explained that he owned part of a family farm and knew all about the farming and ranching business. He had worked on the Railroad in Kansas. He went on to explain that he had learned tailoring when he was in the war and had also owned and operated a thriving shop in Kansas City. He also told Flynn that he was able and willing to learn anything he could about the lumber business. "Well, John, be here at 6 A.M. on Monday mornin'. This will give you a couple days to get settled in. Look for me. I'll be around this area someplace." Flynn, then went on to talk to the other guys.

John was just about to get on his horse when he spotted two guys walking toward him. He stopped and asked them if they knew where he could find a house to rent and also a place to house his life stock. They didn't know of any place but they knew of a guy that might be able to help him. John spent most of the afternoon checking on places. Toward evening, he was getting discouraged and tired. He was about to give up and go back to camp when a burly sort of man came up to him on the street.

" My name is MacDonald. Most people call me Mac. Are you John Taylor?"

"Yes I am." John answered while shaking the man's hand.

"Well, I'm hearing that you just arrived bringin' in that wagon train. Have you had any luck findin' livin' quarters? I hear you might need somethin'."

"I sure do! Been walkin' the town over lookin'. Haven't found what I need. I have a good sized family and livestock to house."

"Grab your horse and ride along with me. I might have what you are lookin' for. I have a house and several acres. I have them up for rent but I want to sell them. Might be just what you are looking for."

They rode on for about thirty minutes. Mac lead John down a long roadway which took them into a large yard which surrounded a large two story white wood framed house with a large front porch.

'This looks great' John thought to himself. 'Hope it isn't too expensive.'

Mac got off his horse and John followed. Tying the horses up, they went inside entering a large kitchen.

"Jane, my wife would love this. All the cabinets and big windows." John commented. They wandered into a large living room. The big windows overlooked the large lawn area and the evergreen trees. The beautiful cedar trees seemed to be everywhere among the giant firs. It made a beautiful picture. The pasture lands were just beyond this.

On the far wall was a set of stairs leading to the bedrooms above. John followed Mac. The large windows were in each room of the four bedrooms. The house was huge. John was getting more excited the more he looked. 'I have to have this house. Jane and the kids would be happy. Hope he doesn't want to much for it.' he thought.

Riding around the property, he saw the large pasture land with the corrals and the creek running through it. John had made up his mind. "Mac, what exactly are you askin' for all of this as far as sellin' goes? Guess you know that I would like to have it. It just seems to be what we need. I do have some money." Soon John and Mac had made a deal. John would end up owing Mac a few hundred dollars but it wouldn't take long to pay that off, now that John was starting a new job at the lumberyard. They would be meeting to sign the papers and finish the deal in the morning.

John was so excited he could hardly wait to get back to camp and tell Jane and the kids. He rode his horse fast and hard to get there. Jumping off his horse, he grabbed Jane and swung her around. The kids came running from all directions. "Everybody, sit down! I have something' really important to tell you! Hurry up!" He grabbed Isabel and put her on his knee. " I got a job today at the lumberyard. Bob introduced me to a Mr. Flynn. He is the foreman there and apparently does the hirin'. I was told to be there Monday mornin'."

Jane jumped up and gave him a big hug. The relief seemed to take her over and tears came to her eyes. The news was so wonderful. John stood up and put his arm around Jane and while still facing the kids, he said "I have more news! I spent most of the afternoon lookin' for a place to live. Nobody seemed to have anythin' or know of any place. I was gettin' discouraged and very tired. I was about to come back to camp when a fellow by the name of Mac came up to me and introduced himself. He said that he had heard I was lookin' for a place and he had somethin' that I might be interested in and would I care to ride with him to see it."

"Well, we rode for about half an hour. He showed me the most beautiful two story, four bedroom house you have ever seen. It has a large barn, a few acres of pastureland with a creek runnin' through it and a large grassed lawn. You just have to see it!"

Everybody grabbed their dad and hugged him. They were so excited and happy that they were all asking questions at the same time. Kathleen asked, "When will we be movin' everythin' there?" Her and the other kids were tired of the wagon. They were thrilled and were ready to do what ever was necessary to get into their new home.

"We will leave camp tomorrow mornin' when I return from meetin' with Mac and finishin' our business. Right now I am so tired and hungry that I'm goin' eat and go straight to bed." Jane handed him a plate of ham and beans that she had cooked up earlier. The kids were sent to bed with the promise that they would have their very own beds tomorrow night.

MOVIN' IN

W hen John got to the long road that led to the house, he stopped. He looked at the eager faces of his family and felt so proud of them and so happy that he could do this. "Get goin', Dad! Don't stop here! Hurry up!" The kids were very anxious to get there.

Moving on, John pulled the wagon up to the big front porch. The older kids scrambled out the back of it, taking the younger ones with them and Jane climbed off the high wooden seat. They hurried inside to see their new home, running through the house and outside into the yard.

John brought them all together in their new kitchen. "I have to go back to camp and get the supply wagon and the livestock. Bill, you can go along with me. The rest of you help your mother unload the wagon into the house."

Turning to Jane, he told her that he would be back as soon as he could. It would take most of the day to get the livestock separated and herded home. Bill would drive the supply wagon. John would ask a couple of the guys from camp to come along and help herd. It would be a hard day and they were looking forward to the days end. After John and Bill unharnessed the wagon and Bill had taken the oxen to the pasture, John got on his horse and pulled Bill up behind him. They would ride back to camp double.

The camp was a buzzing hive of activity. He spied Lars and Erma in a group. Everyone was busy getting their wagons ready to move or working their livestock or just plain standing around. It was plain that the camp was breaking up.

Walking up to them, Lars asked John and Bill, "Where are Jane and the kids?"

"Left 'em at the house unloadin' the wagon. We are here to get the livestock and the supply wagons.

Suppose that I could get a couple of you to help me herd? Maybe we can trade help?" John asked.

"We want everyone in the camp to meet at our place on Saturday for a real get together. Lars, I'll give you the directions so you'll know where to find us. Maybe you can pass the word to the others. If we can do anythin' to help, all you have to do is ask. That goes for everybody." Soon they were moving slowly down the road towards their new home. They would bring the herd the long way around the town, rather than the short way through it.

Something spooked a steer and it started to run the other direction, exciting the other cattle and the oxen. John lassoed it from one side and another lasso landed on it from the other side bringing the steer to it's knees. Soon it calmed down and the ropes were removed. The day was hot and sultry. They wouldn't have water until they got to the pasture. It was decided to let them rest for a little while and give them a chance to relax. They didn't want a stampede on their hands. Shortly before dark, they herded the livestock into the corrals and locked the gates. Bill drove the wagon up to the back porch and left it until morning. He un-harnessed the oxen and headed them back to the corral. "We'll leave 'em 'til mornin'. Can't do much more tonight. Come on in and have somethin' to eat."

"Guess not! It's getting' dark. We'll be headin' back to camp. Have a lot to do tomorrow. Thanks anyway."

John stood with his arm around Bill and thanked the guys. He told them that they were looking forward to seeing them on Saturday. Jane was waiting for them. She found kindling and fire wood on the back porch and built a fire in the large black cook stove that stood in the kitchen. She had warmed up some food. They sat down at some boxes and ate.

"Guess we'll have to see about getting some furniture in the next couple of days. I put the kids all to bed on the floor. They are a happy bunch. I think they were all asleep soon as I left 'em." Jane commented.

"Where do you want me?" Bill asked. "I'm tired out and I don't think it will take me long to fall asleep either."

Jane pointed upstairs and told him, "I made your bed. You'll sleep in Isabel and Nancy's room tonight. Later on we'll figure the bedrooms out."

Bill was half way up the stairs before his mother was through talking. He was headed for bed.

Jane put her arms around John. "Let's go out on the porch for a few minutes. I know you're tired but it is such a pretty night."

Taking Jane's arm, they went outside. The moon was big and yellow. It sent a lot of light down on the yard and the tired happy couple.

They stood there for several minutes just looking at the yard and hearing the livestock in the background. "We are very lucky people. Look what we have accomplished in our married life. Healthy kids. You and I are healthy. We are all happy." Jane said. " And I'm three months with another child. He or she should be born around the last of March."

"Why didn't you say somethin?" John asked very surprised as he took her in his arms and held her. "How are you feelin'? You should have said somethin.' What

197

if you would have had problems out there some place on the trail?"

"You had enough to think and worry about without worryin' about me. I've been feelin' okay. I didn't want you to have to keep checkin' on me. Besides, what could you have done about it if I had problems?" Giving him a big kiss, she went on, "We'll tell the kids later when the house is in order and we can relax a little bit."

"Guess we'll have to consider more fences around the property. Maybe take down some trees." John said to Bill. "We can order the posts from Flynn down at the lumberyard."

John liked his job there. When they heard that he could sew a straight seam, they figured that he could cut a straight line so he was taught to use the saws. He became a sawyer and this became his job.

They had spent the day marking off the property boundary. They planned on starting putting in posts as long as the weather stayed nice. They had some rain but nothing that kept them from working outside. Giving up working at dark, they went into the house. Jane had furnished it from the kitchen through the upstairs. She had gone shopping and found the nicest beds and dressers. Going to another shop, she found a large overstuffed divan and two matching chairs. She then found odds and ends of tables and lamps. She was so glad that she had talked John into bringing the large oak table and chairs from Kansas. This made the house into a comfortable home.

Walking into the kitchen, they could smell the fresh bread and food. They were hungry and could hardly wait to eat. They walked to the basin that sat on a small table beside the back door and washed their hands.

"How was your day?", he asked Jane as he gave her a big hug.

"Bessie has been sick all day. She gets feverish then cold. Nothin' I do seems to help her. She hasn't been able to eat. I fixed her soup but she couldn't hold it down. Think you should go for the doctor? I'm real worried about her." she answered.

"Doctor Stone is right downtown so it won't take me long to get there."

Turning to Bill, he said, "how about goin' out and saddlin' up the mare. Then you can eat."

Within thirty minutes John was on his way and within an hour he had returned with the doctor.

"She has pneumonia! I wish I could give you better news than this." the doctor said after examining her. "You'll have to keep her very warm and greased down. I'll give her some tablets that might help. Hopefully we can break the fever before mornin'. I'll stay here tonight in case she needs me." "John, go to bed for a while." Jane said. "You look worn out. If anythin' changes, I'll wake you up. The doctor is here. Not much more we can do. "

"I'll just lay down for awhile and then I'll relieve you. You need to rest too." John answered. "We have to think about the unborn too."

John woke up and it was daylight. Nobody had come to wake him. He jumped out of bed and hurried to Bessie's room. Jane and the Doctor were talking outside the room. "There hasn't been any change." Doctor Stone said. "I can't understand it. The fever should have come down in the night."

Looking at Jane, he told her to go to bed for a while. "You are very tired and in your condition, you can't get sick too. Now I insist that you lay down."

John went looking for Kathleen. She would help him get breakfast and feed everyone.

Breakfast was about over, when the doctor called down from the top of the stairs.

John and Jane both ran to Bessie. "Her fever has broken. She seems better. She'll be in bed for about a week then she has to build her health up again. She will always be sickly. You will just have to be there for her."

The relief was over whelming and Jane sat down and cried.

Immediately she started washing Bessie down and put a clean night gown on her. She felt cool to the touch. She gave her a big hug and let her go back to sleep. What a relief!

BESSIE

It had been a hard rainy cold winter. John and Bill had put up fence posts and strung fencing around the property. In a few more days, the property would be completely fenced in and the livestock would have the run of the land.

They were busy working, when Kathleen came and got them. "Mom is goin' to have her baby. Come quick, Dad. Hurry! Someone will have to go fetch the doctor. "

"Bill, saddle up and go get Doc Stone. Tell him to come right away!" John told Bill.

John took Kathleen by the arm, and they hurried back to the house. They found Jane walking around, holding her stomach and gasping for breath.

"I don't think it will be very long now." Jane commented.

"How long has this been goin' on?" John asked. "You should have sent for me sooner."

"Nothin' you could do but worry and walk the floor with me. It will probably be a few more hours before anythin' happens.

"I'm carryin' this one a little bit different from the way I was with the girls. I'm thinkin' we'll have us another boy. Bill would have a brother." Jane said. "But don't depend on it. It could still be a girl."

"Either way is okay with me." John said as he watched her walk from room to room.

"I think it is comin'," Jane said. "I'm goin' up to my room so I can lay down if I have to. I'll wait for Doc Stone there."

John went to the door and looked out. Although not much time had gone by since Bill went after the doctor, he wanted him to be there. 'Won't be long now and they'll be here' he thought. 'They'll hurry!'

Going upstairs to be with Jane, he left Kathleen to bring the doctor up as soon as he arrived.

It seemed like no time at all and the doctor was there. Coming into the bedroom, he set down his black medical bag and took off his hat and coat.

"How are you doin'?" he asked. "Is it time yet? How far apart are the pains? How are you feelin'?" He asked John to leave the room while he examined her. " I took the liberty to send for Mrs. Larson to help me as midwife. She tells me that you are friends." "I don't think it will be long now, doctor. He wants to be here." Jane answered. "You are really sure it's a boy this time. Maybe you are right."

"The Larson's came with us from Kansas. Thanks for askin' Erma to come." Jane thanked him.

John knocked at the door. He had Erma with him. About this time Jane screamed and the doctor sent John and Kathleen out of the room. "Wait outside. We'll let you know when somethin' happens." he then examined Jane again. Then he went downstairs and had coffee with John. Erma came downstairs and got him. The baby was coming. The doctor headed upstairs with John right behind him. Their son Joseph joined the family March 27, 1889. The girls wanted to hold him and they were told that they could after a while. John held his son and again thought of Tommy in Kansas.

Soon the family was back to their usual routine. Poor Bessie always seemed to be out of breath. The doctor called it asthma. Sometimes it was very hard to watch her. They tried not to excite her. This seemed to bring on an attack.

Work seemed to slow down at the lumber yard. John heard that the Northern Pacific railroad was looking for engineers for a new line that they were going to run from Tacoma to Puyallup to the coal mining towns of Buckley, Wilkeson and Carbonado in the mountains. John talked to the Railroad people and since he had some experience with railroad work, he was hired. They would start him learning the job from the ground up, starting as a fireman on the Tacoma to the Everett run. While doing this, he was also learning to be an engineer. He learned fast and liked his work. It wasn't long before he was engineering a train round trip between the mining towns and Tacoma. He loved to control the train and blow the whistle.

Bessie was getting sicker and sicker. Doc Stone had heard about a specialist from back east that had started a practice in Seattle. He told Jane and John about him. It was decided that Jane would take Bessie and go see him.

The doctor made a careful examination. He was very concerned.

"Will you leave Bessie with me and my wife for a few days so I can observe her?" he asked Jane. "I think that her immune system isn't working properly."

Jane agreed to this. She wanted what was best for Bessie. She was so sick and there wasn't much else that could be done.

Three days later, Jane went to the doctor's to bring Bessie home. After sending Bessie into the other room to wait, he set Jane down. "I wasn't able to learn much. During my studies, I learned that certain foods and plants brought on asthma attacks." He then gave her a list of foods for Bessie not to eat and also plants that she shouldn't be around.

Everything was tried. All house plants were removed and spicy foods, milk products and other foods were taken from her diet.

One morning Bessie didn't come down to breakfast with the other kids. Jane asked where she was and the answer was that she was still asleep. Jane hurried to the room that Bessie shared with Nancy. Her heart was in her throat. She tried to wake her but she couldn't. The little eight-year old had died in the night on October 23, 1890.

The sadness shook the household. They knew she was very ill but it was still a shock. People came from all over to the services. John and Jane thought again about their boy in Kansas. Bessie and Tommy would be together and Bessie wouldn't hurt anymore. Time went by rapidly over the next three years. Their son Walter was born March 15, 1891 and their son Daniel was born February 21, 1893. The family liked their new home and felt very comfortable in the environment. The people were friendly. The family grew and thrived. They never regretted leaving Kansas.

JOHN

A panic had taken over the country and left everyone in a national financial depression.

Money was short. People weren't spending like they had been. The opportunists had packed up and left. The population fell as thousands of people left the area to find work else where.

A nice warm breeze was blowing, not a cloud in the sky. John found Jane in the back yard hanging clothes on the clothes line. Walking up to her, he said. "come sit down for a minute." Leading her to a wooden chair, and sitting down in another chair beside her, he continued. "I haven't been feelin' well. I went by and seen Doc Stone. He checked me out and drew some blood out of my arm. I know you have been after me

209

to do this but I really thought I had a cold and it would get better."

Jane sat looking at him with a look of dismay on her face. "Oh, John!" she said. "What in the world did Doc Stone find out?"

"He isn't absolutely sure yet but he thinks it is consumption. My lungs are in very bad shape and it is getting' harder for me to breathe."

"The time is coming when we will have to sell off everythin' here and move to town. I won't be much help and it's too big for you and the kids to run yourselves.

"I've given this a lot of thought. I want to sell everythin'. The land and the cattle and all house hold thin's we won't be needin'. I found a place in town not far from the water that we can rent. It is on a corner. Has a large area down stairs for a shop and a large livin' quarters upstairs. We can open up the tailor shop again. I will work as long as I can."

"As always, John you seem to have everythin' under control. You know it's okay with me." "What does the Doc say about you gettin' well? What can he do for this?" she asked in a scared voice.

"I just have to take it easy and not work so hard. Not much more can be done." he answered as he got up and went to her. Kneeling down, he just reached out his arms and held her. They stayed like this for several minutes.

"You remember my brother Ed? I've written to him, over in Montana. You know that he never married. Says that he wants you and the kids to come. He lives in the mountains and has a lot of land for the kids to run on. He has run sheep for years and is quite wealthy. If somethin' should happen to me, he wants you to sell everythin' here and take the kids and go to him. He will help you and the kids. Please promise me that you will do this."

"Of course! If this is what you want. Oh, John! Isn't there somethin' that we can do to make you well? Isn't there somewhere you can go and get help?" Jane was trying very hard to keep from crying. She knew that this would upset John. She had to keep calm and strong for John and the kids.

"Nothin' can be done. You have to keep strong for everybody. We'll sell everythin' we can and when the time comes, you and the kids can leave for Montana and Ed." John went back into the house and Jane went back to hanging clothes. The tears were flowing down her cheeks and she prayed for help for John and that she would be able to carry through with what he wanted her to do. She knew she had the help of the kids.

John found a buyer for the place. He sold the cattle and machinery with the land. This made it much easier to move into town and set up the tailor shop. It was a very busy time. Many trips had been made into town, moving equipment and large house hold items and getting them set up. Moving day at last arrived for the remaining household goods. The shop was at last set up and ready to open.

John had been getting sicker and sicker each day. They had only been in town a couple of months when John became so ill that he couldn't get out of bed. Jane closed up the shop and devoted her time to caring for him and the kids.

One morning when Jane was taking John his breakfast, she pushed the door open and started toward the bed with the tray of food. She started to tell him good morning when she realized that he didn't look right. Setting down the tray on the night stand, she went to the bed. Shaking John's shoulder, she said "Good morning!" But John didn't answer. He had passed away.

Jane sat on the bed and held John's head in her lap. She sat for a long time. Finally she got up and went downstairs and asked Bill to go for the doctor. She took him aside and told him that it was very urgent that Doc Stone come immediately. She chose not to tell Bill everything right away. Why cause him any more pain until she had to. She would gather all the kids to her after Doc Stone left and explain everything to them.

As Doc came through the door, he handed his hat to Kathleen and went on to John's room. Jane was setting on the bed. She had just bathed John.

"How are you?" he asked her. He took her in his arms and held her. Gently setting her back on the bed he went to John and checked his pulse. He pronounced him dead. Looking at his watch, he wrote the time down on the piece of paper he had taken from his bag.

"Let's see today is January 16, 1895", he said as he continued writing.

"We have known this would happen. He has been in pain for a long time and now he is at peace. What will you and the kids do now?"

"I promised John that I would sell the shop. The kids and I will go to Montana to his brother Ed. John made the arrangements. Guess we will do this as soon as I can settle things here. John left us very well off so I don't have to worry about money." Jane answered.

"This is great. It would be hard here with the economy the way it is and harder still for a widow lady with a family."

"If there is anything that I can do just let me know. You, John and the family have always been friends to everyone." He picked up his bag and left.

Jane sent Kathleen to get the kids and they gathered around her at the big oak table. It was a very sad time. They had been through some sad times but this was their father.

Daniel and Walter didn't seem to understand and just asked questions about it. Jane explained that they would be moving to Montana to see their uncle Ed. The children were excited to go but wanted to stay too. They had heard so many stories about Montana and the mountains from different people that had come from there.

The time seemed to pass quickly. Jane sold all the shop equipment and the larger household items but couldn't bring herself to sell the large oak table and chairs. These along with smaller items such as clocks and etc. were shipped to Montana along with the kids clothes and essentials. These items would go as freight on the same train as the family would be riding.

At last the day arrived and Bill brought the buckboard around to the front of the building. Jane helped all the kids on and got them settled for their trip to the railroad station. Looking back she smiled and said "Well, John, you are sending us on another adventure. You will always be with us and we will always remember you."

ABOUT THE AUTHOR

Veda Taylor Strong was born Veda Ellen Taylor in Harlowton, Montana, a small town in central Montana. She was the tenth child of eleven children. She later graduated from Stanford high school, another small town close by. She lived in Great Falls, Montana until she married and moved to Houston, Texas. This didn't work out and she returned home to Great Falls. In 1962, she remarried. In 1967 she moved with her husband and two small boys to Bremerton, Washington. Here she has made her home with her husband and family.

She has worked as real estate agent, bartender, waitress, school custodian, Notary Public and apartment manager. She enjoys working with the public and the elderly.

Her hobbies are crossword puzzles, genealogy, reading and writing. She has always had a strong urge to write a book.